Copyright © 2017 Brian F Freeman

All rights reserved

AUTHOR'S NOTE

Although The Forty Elephants and Alice Diamond did exist, this book is essentially a work of fiction. All other characters, events and situations portrayed in the story are fictitious. Any similarity either in text or image to real persons, living or dead is coincidental and not intended by the author.

No part of this book may be reproduced, or stored in a retrieval system, or transmitted in any form or by any means, electronic, mechanical, photocopying, recording, or otherwise, without the express written permission of the publisher.

The language and attitudes in the book reflect the era in which the story is set.

THE FORTY ELEPHANTS

by

Brian F Freeman

Chapter 1

It is the present day.

An elegant well-dressed woman is standing in Oxford Street holding the hand of a young girl who is equally well dressed. The woman's face shows lines around the eyes of a person that's had a hard life but at the same time likes a laugh. Through her eyes, the atmosphere is silent. She slowly surveys the scene from her vantage point opposite a large crowd that is heaving, pushing towards the doors of a large department store. She smiles; the low rumbling of people filters into her mind, the child grips her hand tighter at the noise, getting louder. She notices the stern security staff, the police getting quietly agitated, the pushing and shuffling increasing. The child looks up to her. She pulls her closer as the atmosphere gets more intense.

The younger security staff faces register panic and frustration. The chimes of a clock bell announces nine o'clock. The woman and child both look to see the source of the chiming a few blocks up the road. The clamour has now risen to a crescendo, the doors are opened, the crowd rushes forward, no questions given, none asked. Old and young push forward like a rolling tide. The police security force stands back to let the stampede stream through the various doors, then up to spread through all the departments. The woman smiles again.

"What's all the rush for, Grandma? Is everything going to be free?"

Laughingly "Not quite, Dolly."

"Can we go inside? It looks like fun."

"Not at the moment. We'd get lost in the crush."

"Maybe later?"

"Certainly, on our way back."

They stay on the opposite side of the road for a time until the crowd diminishes.

"It's free and for nothing?"

"Not quite everything, Dolly, but some things are."

The girl's gaze shifts to a group of young women forcing their way out of the doors, pushing everybody in their path out of the way.

"Grandma, why are those ladies pushing people like that? It's very rude, isn't it?"

1930 - THE PEABODY BUILDINGS, WATERLOO

A group of women are in a state of undress. They are giggling, posing in front of large moveable mirrors. They hang their dresses over tailor's dummies. One of the women gets hold of one of the dummies, embraces it, forcing it backwards trying to get her leg over. The entourage squeals with laughter.

"Can't you wait till you get home?"

"You lecherous bitch!"

"If only Albie could see you now!"

She is helped to her feet, one of the women helps her into a specially tailored dress that had hidden pockets. Another woman was busy pulling up a pair of knickerbockers, were voluminous, a pair of hands helped her put on a dress, similar to all the other dresses. Letting her breath in, she slowly pulls the zip up the back to her neck.

This operation of completion took half an hour. When they had finished, a bottle of whisky was produced and their glasses topped up.

"Now girls, only one. We must all be on our best behaviour, mustn't we?"

This was another excuse for them to laugh.

"Certainly. We don't want to make a spectacle of ourselves, do we, girls?"

More laughter

"Now if we all go into the back room, there are some cummerbunds, muffs and hats. They are all turned inside out so that you can see the pockets and memorise them. Speed and concealment is for the success of the operation."

The atmosphere is ghost quiet as the girls inspect their attire of concealment. Once they have decided on their attire, they pose once more in front of mirrors helping each other out to smooth out any creases in their garments.

"Okay girls, stand in a line for inspection."

The girls shuffle into a line suppressing their nervous giggles, holding their breaths, biting their lips.

"Now, this is serious, girls."

She reaches for the large hat on Rose's head, a long hair pin is extracted.

"That's what I like to see. Be well prepared."

Giving Rose a small kiss on the cheek, she continues her short walk down the line, nodding her head in approval.

"Okay, all shipshape, now you know the drill, when I give the signal, you go hell for leather, get the best merchandise, don't get caught."

"Okay, Alice." They all chorused together.

"I do love the January Sales!" Alice shouted.

TWO MONTHS EARLIER AT A PUB IN SOUTHAWK

A large group of men are sitting around a large table drinking, being boisterous. That is until Albert, a large built man walks along the edge of the table running his forefinger along the back of each chair. Without any command or signal the room goes quiet, he proceeds to the empty chair that's situated in an alcove facing the group. Albert is the leader of the "Elephant Boys". He looks around at the group.

"Well boys, business is good. Everybody's happy..."

He waits for all their nods of approval, they all tap the table.

"Our friends in the constabulary are all being looked after, turning up just five minutes after we've finished conducting our business."

They all laugh.

"I've taken it on board to donate £200 for the police federations orphanage fund and just for an added sweetener, I have chucked in another £100 for the kids Christmas party, which was well received. Bernard, any other business?"

Sitting beside Albert is a bespectacled balding middle aged man. Reaching down beside his chair, he proceeds to place a large doctor's bag on the table. From this, he extracts a large ledger which he opens. "Yes, it has come to our attention that we have serious competition..."

He looks to his mentor who smiles, encouraging him to continue.

"The name of the gang is the Forty Thieves, or in some quarters the Forty Elephants."

He looks up to see that he has the full attention of his audience, he pauses to get the best effect.

"They are a group to be reckoned with, make no mistake and deserve our full respect. Obviously they are in deep competition with us and have to be nipped in the bud before the police start challenging our reputation, which we can't afford to happen. We have the protection from the old bill up to a point but could lose it if we're not careful."

He looks to Albert then sits down. Albert looks around the table. The group start to mutter amongst themselves. He lets them carry on for a few seconds.

"Right, boys. Any questions? One at a time."

Archie: "How come we've not heard of them on our patch? I've got squealers all over the place, I'd know if anyone farted if they didn't ask me."

There's laughter

Norman: "What about reputations here? We can't lose face."

Tommy: "Has anybody met them here yet?"

There's a resounding "No".

Peter: "So boss, what do you suggest we do, get tooled up, meet 'em and finish them off?"

Albert: "Now that's why we've gone this long without too many problems, I figure it first, all the pros and cons, no violence, if we can help it, keeps everything low key. The old bill are happy, we're happy, right? Right, now what I propose to do is to have a parley first with 'em, see if we can work something out."

Archie: "How'd they get the name "Forty Elephants" or what's the other name? "Forty Thieves"?"

Bob: "Ali Baba got his old lady in the family way, she was catholic."

That suggestion broke the ice. There was a chorus of laughter, followed by a pause of silence.

Bernard looks around the table, takes a mouthful of his whisky uses a napkin to wipe his lips. "Do you realise not one of you have asked what kind of gang they are? Their methods, their backup, how they fence their loot, their getaway, where they carry out their ill gotten deeds..."

There is a snigger of laughter from several of the entourage, but then Albert's silence is observed straight away.

"Right, 'ere it is, our 'Forty Thieves' are a bunch of ladies, but not quite ladies as what you lot are used to."

The whole group look at one another dumbfounded.

"These ladies are the most hardened women I have ever come across, and they are clever, charming, well educated in the art of making money, and above all, they're fucking hard. Their governor, well, let's put it like this, I wouldn't fancy my chances meeting her in a dark alley on my own."

They all burst out laughing, one man exclaiming "I bet you would if you had your cock out!"

Albert: "I'm deadly serious, I'm gonna have a meeting with her to see if we can work together…"

Archie: "What's her name? Jack Johnson?"

Albert: "No. Alice Diamond. But to us and the old bill, they call her "Diamond Annie"."

THE NEXT DAY

West End Central Police Station, 7.30am

Four detectives are loosely seated around the detective sergeants table. They are talking, considering the information on a blackboard supported with an old fashioned school easel the d/s is the first to speak.

"Now we've got a grass inside the "Elephant Boys" gang as you know they're getting quite busy as of late. They've started a protection racket in Lambeth, but this on the face of it seems a bad decision."

He goes to the board and starts to chalk up "The Elephant Boys". As he goes to underline the name, he pushes down too hard on the chalk. It makes a screeching noise then breaks.

"Jesus, go easy guv! That makes my orchestra stalls tighten!"

They all chuckle

"You just like when it's your turn to get a round in."

"Pity that's where your brain is."

"That's enough. Pay attention..."

He draws a circle with the chalk, then extends four lines coming off the perimeter then starts to chalk some information.

"They have had a bit of a run in with a North London gang, so to keep a low profile they got involved with another gang."

He turns to print the name "The Forty Elephants"

The atmosphere quickly changes to silence. He had their full attention.

"I thought that might interest you. This is a gang we've never come up against..."

He goes to the board again, his back hiding what he is about to chalk. He then turns to face them, moves out of the way, one word is underlined "Women".

"What's that all about then, guv?"

"Well, we ain't got much info at the moment, but what I do know is we might have our work cut out if we don't nip this in the bud..."

One of the detectives ventured "Well, what's the problem? What can a bunch of women do to make our job any harder?"

"This bunch of women, namely over thirty, go into a top department store in the West End, let's say Derry & Toms, right, it's planned like a military operation. They would enter through numerous entrances in groups of three or four to confuse the staff and store detectives; they would pilfer what they wanted before moving out en masse..."

"Hang on a minute, how could they carry the loot without being seen?"

The D/S starts to draw a rough sketch of a women's dress. He looks round to the quizzical looks on their faces, smiles, then turns back to the board again. He then proceeds to chalk large square pockets on the dresses.

"Inside these pockets, they put the spoils. Small expensive items, watches, jewellery, folded up dresses anything they can fence to make it worth their while."

"What if one of the girls were caught? It wouldn't be hard to arrest them."

"It's not as easy as that. They round on the would-be hero; punching, kicking... also they've got this bleeding vicious use of a large pin that they keep in their hats. That comes out, it takes a brave man who doesn't want to be blinded or worse, to let 'em go. Once in the street, they have a small fleet of cars to piss 'em off into the sunset."

One detective asks "So who's bank rolling them? What's in it for them?"

"Well, my grass tells me it's the Elephant Gang, always on the lookout for an easy way for a penny to be earned. It looks an easy touch. The women take all the risks, sell all the loot to them at knock down prices, they fence the proceeds, everybody's 'appy. Now you may think they can't get much of the schmuter out. They fill their dress pockets to the hilt. High class garments, good quality jewellery watches, anything small, expensive... I've had it from the top that this little enterprise is to be nipped in the bud."

There is a brief pause, and then one of the detectives speak up.

"Where do we fit in, guv?"

"Right, I need one of you to infiltrate the group, be accepted, work with one of the girls, find out all the angles, their strategy... Remember these ain't country girls. The whole shebang is run like a bleeding military operation, so it ain't gonna be a tea party. I've got some folders on the desk, so read 'em thoroughly. Don't take 'em out of the room! Tomorrow, I'll interview each of you individually to see if you want to be considered for the job."

He rubs all the relevant chalk images off the board, the group all look at one another, then scanter over to the desk, each picking up a file, find a place to read the contents, all in silence.

Two days later: 8:30am

A small convoy of three cars drive round the Elephant and Castle roundabout. The cars sublime in their appearances, keeping well in the accepted speed limit. The driver is dressed as a chauffeur, peaked cap black livery, all the occupants are women, conspicuous of the time of wearing hats. The cars make their way along Blackfriars Road, over the bridge, moving onto Kings Cross. Here, they break the chain, letting one or two cars get in between them, so as not to create any suspicion as they head up Marylebone Road towards Oxford Street. They start to adorn their hats taking extra care that the lethal hat pins are well and truly embedded in the material with just the bobble head of the pin protruding.

The cars slowly turned down the street going to the bottom of the street, making sure the cares were backed up but with enough room in between just in case one of them got boxed in, or failed to start. As they got out of the cars, they started to talk to one another, at the same time adjusting their dresses so that the pockets in their dresses were open, and their oversized knickerbockers were unstretched, patting the front of the dresses down, they then adjusted their hats to proceed to the small side entrances of "Selfridges".

At the front of the store in Oxford Street, the crowds were pushing and jostling to get the best position, when the doors opened, the public could race to the departments that they had monitored earlier in the week to the objects first; the "Forty Thieves" made a point of keeping close together making it very obvious when anybody tried to break up their group they would blatantly push the person away, not caring if they fell over or got squashed, a sharp kick in the ankles made the point, a sharp dig in the ribs with a hefty elbow left nothing to chance. If this failed, a pulled up brolly in the back gave the required message.

The chimes on the ornamental clock struck nine. The doors opened inwards, the customers surged forward, the scream of shoppers acted as the perfect cover for the "Forty Thieves" camouflaging their act of wholesale thieving.

At the same time, the side doors of stairs were opened this was the signal for other half of the gang to continue their enterprise. In two or three minutes, the store was jam packed with people pushing one another to get to their cherished bargains. No quarter was given and certainly none was asked. It was pure uncontrolled bedlam. Still keeping tightly knitted at the main entrance, the gang made their way to the jewellery department, the side entrance gang went to the designer clothes department, splitting up, they went to the fur department, then on to the lingerie and leather goods.

Alice in her glory, the jewellery counter was a throng of thieving pushing punters, just what Alice wanted, barging through to the front counter. Making sure her entourage is with her, she gets the attention of the young nervous sales lady.

"Yes, dear, could you please show me that ring on the tray down there?"

Pointing to display tray of semi-precious diamond rings, the accomplices have now formed a barrier between the counter keeping the public behind them. The assistant puts the tray on top of the cabinet.

"Could I try that one?"

"Yes, madam."

The tray is now on the counter top, the assistant holding onto it, the group form a circle around Alice who nods to one, who quickly pulls out the pin from her hood then unceremoniously jabs it into the top of the assistant's wrist, with a lengthy scream she instinctively lets go of the tray. Alice quickly puts the tray inside her dress then turns to walk away. To cover her exit, the other members of the gang form a route for her to move into the mainstream. The assistant, who is now trying to compose, is calling for assistance, but to no avail. The vacuum made by the gangs departure is quickly filled by the ordinary shoppers who are not fully aware of the incident and cannot be bothered by the commotion being caused by the assaulted assistant. It was business as usual. Alice beckons the group to follow her to the lift, she pauses to look at the stores indicator at the side of the lift, running her finger down the list she stops at lingerie.

"Ladies, I think we will visit the lingerie department to help the company dispose of their fabulous articles. Are we all in agreement?"

There was a collective answer in one voice.

"Oh yes, Alice! Lead the way!"

One of the girls pushes the button. After a short pause, the elevator doors open. People push their way out and leaves the elevator vacant. The girls follow Alice into the elevator, barring anybody else from entering. As the doors close, one of the gang say in a well educated voice:

"You people are just a bunch of peasants! Why can't you use a bit of decorum? It shows your upbringing!"

The people trying to get in the elevator stop pushing. Leaning their heads, looking at one another in disbelief as the doors close, the entourage burst out laughing.

Rose with her group have made their way to the leather department. This was packed with shoppers holding bags above their heads so that a third party could not relieve them of their promised purchases. The girls look at one another smiling in unison. Nodding their heads, no words were spoken. Like snakes in the grass, the planned attack went into operation – turning sideways they formed a natural small circle, keeping tight, slowly forcing their way to the counter. Much to the amusement of the girls, the shoppers let them through to the counter, where a display of leather goods were soon to go missing to new owners.

"Excuse me, miss, may I have a look at the black crocodile handbag?"

Rose enquired in a well manicured voice.

"This one madam?" The assistant brings the bag over.

"No, the one next to it."

"Certainly."

The assistant turns to get the adjacent bag. There are now two bags on the counter. Behind Rose, the punters are pushing forward and the assistant is getting flustered. Rose is slowly undoing the bag. One of her girls in the group slides up close to her, one of the punters is getting annoyed at not getting the attention she craves, getting into more of a semi-panics she turns to answers the punter's problem. This was what Rose was waiting for. Her compatriot opens her coat putting one of the bags in her extended knickerbockers. Rose likewise opens her coat, sliding the other bag into her knickerbockers. The innocent bystander looks on in amazement at how quickly the two bags vanished. Too late, the assistant turns just to see Rose surrounded by her partner in crime, exiting the department doors. She is in a dilemma – either choose to run to the phone or just carry on serving. Chivalry gets the better of her, she quickly gets to the phone.

Inside the store detectives offices, there are seven men sitting around a table playing cards, the senior detective takes the message, looking around to his colleagues.

"Can you describe them?"

He nods his head as the callers describes them.

"That sounds about right... yes... yes... no, you've done the right thing. Now get back to your post. Well done."

Ending the call, he turns to the others.

"Okay, boys, it looks like the Elephant Gang have arrived. Now go to your positions! I'll get in touch with the heavy mob."

The store detectives take one last puff on their cigarettes. And with their last gulp of tea, chairs are unceremoniously pushed to one side as they scrambled to the door.

Alice with her group have now ascended to the 2nd floor, pushing their way through the punters. They are very well co-ordinated in their manoeuvre. Keeping tightly knit, they enter the lingerie department. Without speaking, Alice gestures to the counter. Pausing, she scans the assistants, always looking for the youngest nervous one. Nodding her head, the same procedure swings into action. Looking from above, it looks like a pride of lions encircling its prey. Pushing through the melee, she waits until the chosen prey catches her eyes. Alice is now at the fore front of the counter which is two feet wide, the top covered in open boxes of lingerie. But this is not what Alice is looking for. Casting her gaze upwards, she recognises her goal. It was the French, Italian, anything continental… The high class and provocative lingerie was her want. The gang inconspicuously kept under their coats, keeping a tight protective ring around Alice, casually looking through the subordinate lingerie.

"Excuse me for being such a pain, but could you show me your continental collection? It would be so much appreciated."

The assistant looks left and right to see if anybody could help, but to no avail. Getting a key from her neck, she reaches up to unlock the special display cabinet, sliding out a long tray to display the goods.

"Thank you, my dear. If you're busy, I'll just have a look at these. They're not for me, you understand."

"Certainly, madam. Would you like to know the price?"

"No, I don't have a problem with that."

Another punter is insisting about the price of the other lingerie, distracting the assistant.

"Don't worry, I'll look through these. You go ahead."

"I hope you realise they are not in the sale?"

"Most certainly."

The assistant is getting more perplexed, the other innocent customer is getting more frustrated that Alice is getting more attention. To make matters worse, another customer tries to take the collection she is holding out of her hand.

"Do you mind? I'm buying these!" She says very briskly.

"Well, where is your money?"

She ventures to ask, sarcastically.

"What? That's got nothing to do with you."

They begin a tug of war over the items, which quickly turns into a small brawl. The assistant now starts to panic and tries to push a help button, then proceeds to walk down to the melee. This was Alice's chance. Her coat opened, her hand quickly shot out, cupping up the whole collection from the tray to find a safe haven in one of the inside pockets of her coat. A woman standing between Alice's accomplices could not believe what she had just witnessed. She tried to shout to get the attention of the assistant, but with a wide opened mouth, no sound came out – seeing the funny side of this, Rita picks up a loose pair of knickers and proceeded to quickly put in to her mouth. Alice witnessed, laughing turned sharply on her heels, followed by her accomplices. Further down the counter, Rita witnesses the act has been a success. She smiles sarcastically at her adversary, letting go of the underwear.

"Mind you, with a boat like yours, you'd need more than these to get your old' man in a frenzy!"

She laughs and pushes her way through the punter to join Alice at the perimeter of the crowd, who are all laughing.

The store detectives run in different directions, trying to head off the gang. Once out into the store, they all look at one another shaking their heads in disbelief. The service counters are chock-a-block with customers more than ten deep, it looked like a thieving mess of snakes, nobody giving ground or asking for it.

"Bleedin' hell, what did they expect us to do here? If you said the place was on fire, you wouldn't budge 'em..."

"Jesus mother of Mary, you'd think this was the last place in London with any soddin' clothes left!"

"Where are we supposed to look for these tarts? They ain't exactly holding a sign saying '"ere we are!"'!"

"Okay, button it! I want each one of you to go to the women's department on the first four floors. The only way to suss 'em out is that they may be a small group walking away from the crowds. Right, they'll have bags full up of merchandise. Don't be afraid of 'em, just collect the one with the biggest bag, she'll spill the beans about the others when we take her down to the office. Right, now sod off and bring back a result!"

The men run off in different directions pushing their way through the crowds. It was a thankless task.

On the second floor, one of the detectives was scanning a group of women laden with bags being far too overzealous. He barges his way through to the group grabbing the woman with the most bags by the wrist. She looks around in utter amazement, then goes on the defensive pulling away but the detective holds on.

"Excuse me madam, I would like you to accompany me to the store detectives office. Bring your bags with you, please..."

The woman had now composed herself.

"I beg your pardon? Show me your identity, and I'll show you my receipts!"

The store detective had to bluff it out. All the time the crowd was squeezing the entourage close together, he gets out his brief pulling above the tightening melee. That was the worst action he could have taken, with all the pushing and shoving it was quickly knocked out of his hand, the women sensing that she had the advantage took the initiative.

"You could be anybody, for all I know! Now be on your way!"

With that, she brought one of the heavy bags down on his head.

On the third floor, Rose decides it's time to vacate. Her minder makes a passage for her exit, their coats are full of items, making it that little bit harder to force their way through the crowd. As they reach the lobby entrance to the elevator, the store detective appears. The gang all look at one another, the guilt is attached on their startled face. The store detective does not know what to do. They are not carrying any of the companies bags. They pause. Hesitation is what Rose needed. She takes the initiative.

"Ah, young man! Could you please take us to the ground floor? I have my chauffeur waiting, and as you know, they can become terribly impatient and huffy."

The store detective stands his ground, pauses, slowly slides his hand to the down button. He looks closest to the left, fixing his gaze, then slowly looks round at the group.

"My servants have a schedule to keep, so could you please take us down or vacate the lift?"

The composure of Rose and her confident voice swings the standoff. The detective nods his head slowly, still not convinced of the situation.

"Yes, madam. I hope you had a good days shopping."

He slowly walks out the lift.

"As you can see, the sales goods were not up to my expectations. I'll return to a more sedate atmosphere when the sale is over. I couldn't abide all this hustle and bustle, you understand."

"Yes, madam."

As they walk past him, he pushes up against Rose's coat; it does not give but has a solid feel about it.

"So sorry, madam. Stand clear of the doors!"

As he leaves, he pushes the button to the ground floor. The group start to laugh but quickly stop as a cache of gloves fall on the floor. Ellie tries to hide them by using her feet.

"Rita, push the button for the second floor!"

Rita quickly obeys, June picks up the gloves putting them in the long pocket of her coat. The elevator stops as they open the door.

"Split up on your own and make your way to the cars in the street!" Rose ordered.

They all leave in different directions down the stairs.

Outside, the detectives from Vine Street have just arrived, jumping out of their cars. They are faced with a human barricade of people trying to force their way through. It was no easy matter. To people who had been patiently waiting, there was no way they were going to let any interlopers pass them, whether shouting they were old bill or not. That was an old ruse.

"Tim, we ain't gonna bluff our way through this bleeding lot!"

"You're right there. Clever sods, aren't they?"

He surveys the scene the chief store detective muscles his way to Tim.

"Glad you could make it. Listen, we're on to a loser 'ere. My boys ain't got a clue. No descriptions, no groups, they planned this like a bleeding military operation."

Tim is still looking around trying to pinpoint anybody who looks suspicious. He is getting pushed and manoeuvred from pillar to post. Rose whose trained eye sees the group before they see her. She made a quick decision. She couldn't turn back as this would cause a situation. She had to just bluff her way through the crowd, turning her face as she walked past Tim. By this time, Sam turned his head, face to face with Rose, and lets her through. She turns behind him in a 'last act of bravado' and speaks quietly:

"Thank you, officer."

Without giving it a second thought, he replies:

"Thank you, madam."

Still not realising the consequences of the remark, he continues forward for several seconds, then it hits. How did she know he was a policeman?"

"Quick, sod it! It's one of them!" He turns to scan the crowd, but it's too late. Rose is out of the entrance making her way to the car. Sam forces his way out to the street; looking up and down, people pushing, women with hats... they are all the same. Breathing in deeply, he saunters back to his leader, sighing.

"You're right, Jim. They're running circles around us. It's like a military operation! How did she know I was a copper? Ugh, right, let's get back inside. We should find out what our store detective friends 'ave gleaned from the operation. For all we know, they could have arrested one with a handful of knickers."

Sam smiles then ponders.

"Jim, if you were in their shoes, how would you make your getaway? It ain't as if they're going to jump on a bus, is it? Or maybe...?"

"Christ, you got a point, they only got one bleeding car! Right, bring all our boys together right away!"

All of the "Forty Thieves" had now gotten all their stolen goods in their coats and were making their way to the allotted sites that had been agreed earlier. The store detectives passed each of the felons but what chance did they have? No descriptions, everybody pushing and shoving, working individually... the odds were well and truly stacked against them.

Rose had now met up with her accomplices. They were waiting in the fire exit doorway of the store, well out of the way of any inquisitive police or store detectives. A low roar coming from Oxford street put them on their guard. Rose gingerly puts her head out and smiles. The car pulls over and the doors are opened by an unseen hand. The girls all giggling jump in, pushing one another around like a Sunday School outing. The high powered car drives off, turning left at the bottom of the road, then taking another left turn back into Oxford Street.

"Well, girls! Alice should be well pleased with our little enterprise! We've all got our bloomers well filled up!"

"Yeah, and it's not with my fiancés ole chap!"

The driver starts to laugh uncontrollably.

"Oi! Keep your concentration on the road! We don't want to end up in St Thomas'!"

All the occupants are now laughing. One of them lowers the window. Pedestrians stand back to let the chariot of joy continue on its journey.

Chapter 2

Back at the store, Alice's group has not been so lucky. The store detectives came down the stairs and looked over the banister. Everybody else was coming up to the next floor, but a group of four women, all well endowed with their 'booty' took up half of the staircase. From their position, it just didn't look right. They both gazed at the scenario, confronting them. Strangely enough, their thought channel connected, looking at one another, they shouted in unison.

"Just a minute, madam! Hold on there!"

Alice's composure stiffened, knowing that if they were apprehended now, they wouldn't stand a chance. Ignoring the challenge, she ushers the group down the stairs, but this time not going towards the entrance of the store, and exiting.

"Follow me, quick!"

She leads them to the basement, a sign above the store states 'Employees only'. They pass through the swinging doors, past startled groups of the company employees. It was the canteen, barging through, knocking over tables, they continued as fast as they could to the next exit. This led to a long corridor. There were only two ways to go. Alice hesitates. Behind them, they hear the pursuing detectives treading on the canteen carnage. Their voices got louder. Alice gestures to the left, up a flight of stairs. They turn once again, one of the group stumbles over her baggage of petticoats and falls into the group. They turn to pick her up, leaving several pairs of underwear that Alice had given to her to hide. She bends to pick them up.

"Leave 'em! The coppers can give them to their birds for a promise."

They laugh nervously. Still in pursuit, the police reach the junction. They stop, but Sam orders two to go to the right while he pursues them to the left, going down the passage, he comes across the underwear. Smiling, he briefly picks them up and put them in his pocket, then continues the chase.

Alice has now led the girls past the last hurdle. It is where a large wall is covered with the clocking-in board. A large clock takes procedure as they run past. Alice flicks down the lever and it reacts with a large ping. The time clerk slides back a glass partition and looks both ways.

"Oi, you can't do that! It ain't time to go!"

"We've just handed in our notice!"

"It sodding well is!" They all laugh.

As they go past, they all flick the lever, laughing. He slams the partition shut and rushes to his door, but to no avail. The group has already vanished.

Up on to the main road, the getaway driver has his engine running. Through his mirror, he sees the group looking up and down the road. He hits the horn and they see him, then run towards him. At the same time, he reverse at full speed, with one hand on the wheel, he leans behind to open the doors, screeching to a halt. The group pile in, and he drives forward before the door is closed. At that same moment, Sam enters the street, just to witness the car turning the corner. The girls wave from the window holding the underwear in the wind. Sam slowly gets out his evidence, looks at it and smiles. Two women from the store come adjacent to him, looking at him incredulously, he offers the underwear to them. They turn their heads, walk two steps forward, pause, then walk back.

"Thank you, but you know those are not for me."

"Of course, madam."

He turns, slowly backs in the direction of the store, the other detectives run towards him, both panting and trying to catch their breath.

"Any luck, Sam?"

"No, clean getaway. All I got of it was two pairs of bras."

They all look at one another and start laughing. Out of sight of the police, the getaway car had just missed a beer-carrying wagon, not having time to swerve, the screech of the skidding tyres spooks the horses. They reared up. The driver had not been able to hold on, and ends up swerving across the road, causing the large beer barrels to fall off, smashing on the cobbles, the contents spilled across the road.

A police car pulls up to Sam.

"Which way did they go?" The driver asked.

"Up the top of the road. Turn left and you might catch 'em."

The police car speeds off, taking the corner at high speed. They were travelling too fast before they were on top of the beer covering the road. They didn't stand a chance. The car skidded in a complete cartwheel, skidding across the road to hit a horse trough, bringing it to an unceremonious halt.

Although the occupants were badly shaken, the police slowly got out of the written off vehicle. Still dazed, they stagger into the deluge of beer, smelling miffed. A crowd quickly gather to witness the incident. The driver has got hold of the reins of the team of horses, trying to soother them down. It was a hard task until they got the scent of the beer. He tries to lead them to the horse water trough, but as they had been reared in the confines of the brewery, their liking to the amber ale was much more to their taste. Shying away from the water trough, they started to drink the ale.

The driver starts to panic and pull at the reins of the horses, but to no avail. Totally perplexed, he gives up in the knowledge that he was not strong enough to pull them away. Admitting defeat, he lets the reins slacken. It was only a matter of time until the great shires would be in a different world and he would be able to lead them to kingdom come and back.

The Detective Sergeant was the next witness to the incident. Luckily the crowd forced the pursuing car to slow down on the blind bend.

The occupants got out, including Sam. Surveying the scene, they all look at the flooded road, then to the drivers holding the two horses who by now were well and truly intoxicated. There was nothing anybody could do. McDonald was the first one to break the stalemate. He turned his back on the scene. The others look over to him. All they could see was his shoulders going up and down controlling a full frontal guffawing. The others could not control themselves so admirably, as they all burst out laughing. McDonald made his way to the car, but could hardly open the door. Then he had lost it. In between gasps, he calls from the car, hardly getting the words out.

"Enough, enough!!"

Slumping forward on the dash board, the other two go over to the driver, who was propped up against the overturned cart. The horses had a dazed look in their eyes, pushing their noses into one another, barely holding his sentences together. Dick approaches the drivers.

"You alright, mate? Is there anything we can do?"

The driver looks at him forlornly.

"Do I look bleedin' alright?! Do you think it's funny?"

The trio burst out laughing again. "Yes!" They exclaimed loudly.

Dick turns and staggers towards the car.

"You two, get a grip! This behaviour won't do our reputation any good!"

"No, guv, I can see it now... 'Police in pursuit of thieves are stopped in their tracks by two drunken horses'!"

This was all that was needed for the whole crew to start laughing uncontrollably as the car slowly pulled away, leaving the carriage driver sitting down, head in hands, with the shire horses licking his head.

Once clear of the store, Rose briskly walked back down Oxford Street to Oxford Circus, keeping close to windows using the reflection to see if she is being pursued. Deciding she was in the clear, she walks over to the curb to hail a taxi.

"King's Cross, please."

Looking through the back window, her face slowly breaks into a confident smile.

"Been doing a bit of shopping at the sales?"

"Yes, I did glance at the entrance but it was so packed with people. I couldn't bear maelstrom of it all. I usually shop at Selfridges two or three times a week and get my goods delivered, but there was no way I was going to get bowed over like a skittle just for the sake of getting five shillings of an item, you understand?"

The driver makes a quizzical look as he glances into his rear view mirror.

"Yes, I understand."

On arrival at King's Cross, Rose pays the cabbie. She goes over the road to go into a public house. At the bar, she orders a glass of Sherry, then enters the ladies toilet. Locking the door behind her, she takes out a square of material that when opened reveals a large carpet carrying bag. From inside her petticoat, she extracts the small items from the concealed pockets, transferring them to the bag. She doesn't got to the bar for her drink but walks out to hail a cab ordering it to "Elephant and Castle".

By now, Alice's car has reached the "Elephant and Castle", all the girls alight, laughing, giggling, then quickly going into a house. Once inside, a long parlour room, they one by one carefully extract all the stolen items onto a long table. They all glance at each other, mulling over their stolen goods, picking them up to see if any of the small items would suit them.

"Well, girls, it's been a good mornings work! You all performed admirably! A couple of close shaves but that goes with the work. Now you know the drill, I'll see you tonight at the "Eagle". Any problems in the meantime, I'll be here waiting for Rose."

Alice slowly goes looking over the goods, picking out a dress, then slowly walks over to a large mirror and hangs it over her shoulders. She smiles, then goes back to the table to pick up an imitation necklace, puts it around her neck, slowly making a pirouette. Pleased with the transformation, she puts the dress back, then goes to pour herself a drink, relaxing on a large chaise lounge, holding the drink up to the light. The stillness is punctured by the phone ringing. Slowly getting up, she picks up the receiver.

"Hello?"

"'ello, Alice, it's Albert. 'eard you and the girls had a nice touch. Alright if I pop over an' scotch the merchandise?"

"God 'elp us, you cotton on so quick. We've only been home ten bleedin' minutes!"

"Never you mind, sweetness, the old bush telegraph 'as its uses."

"Okay, that'll be fine."

"Right, see you in 'alf and hour, ok? I'll knock two taps- then three."

Alice is sleeping on the chaise longe when a tap on the window wakes her. Getting up and peering through the curtains, there is no one there. Just as she is about to turn away, a face pops up. She jumps back and pulls the curtain open again. It's Rose with her smiling face. Alice smiles and lets her in.

"You scared the bleedin' life out of me! Come in here."

Rose enters, setting herself down on the chaise lounge, taking her hat off and throwing her dress in abandonment.

"Oh dear, what a very interesting day I've had..."

"You've had an interesting day? What d'you think I've had? We just about got away without getting our collars felt, I suppose you just walk through all of that with no problem?"

Funnily enough, Alice, I did. And believe it or not, I thanked a police officer. What a wonderful job he was doing..."

"Balls. Now let's 'ave a look at the goods."

Rose slowly gets up to undo her coat to reveal a garment filled with merchandise, putting the contraband on the table. She takes off her dress to reveal a large pair of knickerbockers with pockets chock full of items, then puts them on the table. Alice's smile gets longer by the minute as she surveys the scene before her. For her part, Rose notices the exotic lingerie.

"May I?"

"Of course."

Rose takes off her brassier, but a knock at the door breaks the conversation. Alice puts her finger to her lips. The agreed knocking signal is established. Alice nods her head.

"It's alright, it's only Albert. Coming!"

On opening the door, Albert walks in. Embarrassed, Rose runs behind the large mirror but not before Albert sees her.

"Don't mind me, I'll just watch."

Alice picks up Rose's dress, takes it over, Rose then gets behind the mirror to dress.

Albert's attention is now drawn to the goods on the table. Slowly sifting through the haul, he slowly nods his head, looks to Alice then again to the spread.

"Alice, you've done very well. Much better than I expected."

"Thanks. I've still got four of my other girls to come yet. Their stuff will be just as good."

Rose comes out from behind the mirror, now being suitably dressed.

"It'll be nice of you to model some of these dresses just to see if they fit alright…"

"Albert, how about a drink?"

"Sounds lovely. Alice, what'd I'd like to do is to bring my fence round and give you a price. I don't suppose there is any jeckyls among them?"

"No, they are all genuine."

"Okay, I'll give you a ring later tonight to set up the time. Nice to do business with you, Alice."

He moves forward to kiss Alice, and smiles as Rose leaves.

Scotland Yard

Later that afternoon, the detectives are all gathered at their headquarters. McDonald looks up from his desk.

"Okay lads, pay attention. Obviously you've all witnessed what we are up against. This little group of women ain't no amateurs. They're a pretty slick, well organised operation. The problem we have is…"

He turns to the blackboard, writing down his statement.

"One, we don't know who they are. Two, how many of them are there altogether. Three, how do they get rid of all the merchandise they've nicked. Four, and most importantly, the leader's identity, description, and where they live."

He underlines the last word with a loud dot.

"Right, any suggestions? The commissioner has been breathing down my neck. He wants results and we can't have Oxford Street being taken over by a bunch of women. Not good for the image for tourists and most of all, the tax payers."

There is a pause before he continued.

"Now, I want a couple of volunteers. Anybody got any ideas?"

"Right, I'll enlighten you..."

He turns to the blackboard again. With his back covering what he's writing, he slowly turns to face the others again.

"Can anybody guess?"

He moves away to expose his idea in large letters; "INFILTRATION". He paused again to let the statement sing in, looking around at his men.

"Right, we've got one up on 'em because none of you are known by any gangs at the minute. This'll be our ace up our sleeve. Now I want you all to go outside and I'll call you in one at a time, then I'll decide which one I've chosen. Right, 'way you all go."

The first two who were eliminated because they were married, whittling it down to three. Sam Ford, George Ross, and Shaun Brady. The three detectives were seated around a table, McDonald was seated opposite them, tapping his finger on the desk, the trio are getting a bit uneasy.

"Right, what I propose is this. I just need the two of you to infiltrate the gangs hierarchy. We've already got a move in the Elephant Gang but he's not making any headway. They're a tightly knit bunch and don't take kindly to strangers, especially if you don't originate from around the "Elephant" or Suffolk. Firstly, you gotta understand their mannerisms, lingo, but most of all to carry yourselves as with 'boys'. Your backup stories have to be foolproof. If they find out you're imposters, you'll end up In a wooden overcoat in the isle of dogs or floating in the Thames. You may not think these women are worth the trouble, but they are. It doesn't end there with these shoplifting escapades. If what we believe they've taken is under the wing of the heavy mob, the scenario is they could be engaged in other rackets. They'll get more bolder if we don't collar 'em quick. Now timing is the prime factor. There's gonna be a dog-fighting competition in a week's time in a warehouse down by the Tate and Lyle wharf. Two of you will be there with a dog. If you're squeamish about that, say so now, I'll understand."

He pauses and looks at them one by one.

"Okay, don't mention this conversation to any of the other lads. We'll have another meet tomorrow night down the "eagle" at nine o'clock."

That night, Rose and all the girls are at a house where a large party is taking place. Albert is in deep conversation with Alice.

"Alice, I'm very impressed with your operation. Very slick, fast, and professional. Most of all, nobody got hurt. Y'know, I don't think my blokes could have pulled off what you did today..."

He pauses to let the words of admiration go to their full effect. Alice's face was expressionless. She was a strong character. Dialogue, small talk, and praises didn't mean anything to her. She was as hard as the next man. Albert didn't get the reply he wanted.

"Okay Alice, I'll lay my cards on the table. What I'd like to propose is..."

Alice gave him a quizzical look.

"What I mean to suggest is that with my back-up, putting both our heads together, we could make this into a longer, more profitable enterprise, there's a lot of angles out there which are untapped. I've got some friends in the police force all squared up. I could make it happen that they wouldn't be where you wanted to be, if you see what I mean."

Alice looks at him stone-faced and responds.

"What makes you think I need anybody bustling in my operation? As you saw today, it went quite well. The fences are well pleased with the merchandise."

"I agree with everything you're saying, but what for instance if another gang got to use the same methods on your patch? I could make sure the old bill got to hear about it so there would be no competition. I could get you better prices for your merchandise, faster cars..."

"So what's in it for me and my girls?"

"Well, what I propose is for my protection and everything pertaining what goes on in my manner, I would make a sixty-forty deal..."

"In my favour?"

"No no, Alice. In mine."

At that interjector, Rose slides up to Alice with a drink.

"Champagne for the victor!"

Alice smiles and takes the glass. Albert turns to go.

"You think about it."

"I already have."

Rose then says "Everything alright, Alice?"

"Yes, nothing for you to worry your little head about."

A week later, Sam gets out of a taxi in Jamaica Road, Bermondsey. They have a dog on a lead, walk across the road to the pub, before they enter the public bar, they can hear the baying, barking of dogs. Sam pulls back the lead of his dog straining at the lead on entering the bar. The men playing the piano turn and look them up and down. The other dogs turn, aggressively trying to attack Sam's dog, he pulls the leash shorter.

A bowler hatted man approaches them, eyes them up and down, then looks at his notebook.

"Name?"

"Reynolds." Sam answered.

"Dogs name and age?"

"Satan - two and a half years."

The man lets a wry grin across his face.

"Yeah, right. We've got plenty of his disciples 'ere. We only have a couple rules. You put your money down with Conny 'ere. When the bout's finished, you carry out the cleaning up operation, sharply. We don't want to cause the dogs any unnecessary trauma."

His compatriot smiles, sarcastically nodding his head.

"Okay, get a drink..."

He gets out a pencil, licks the end ticks off the inventory.

"How'd you strengthen his jaws, by the way?"

Sam had to think quick.

"The councils just posted some new monkey bars. I get there early in the morning, hang 'em on a box then pull it away. He 'olds on for dear mercy, a little bit longer each day."

"What about his teeth?"

"I file 'em myself."

The man bends down to take a look. The dog snarls aggressively. Sam makes the leash shorter. Nearly losing his balance, the man jumps back.

"Bastard! I'll believe yuh! I'll have a couple of bob on him m'self."

Albert and his entourage are drinking heavily until a gong shatters the talking. The bowler hatter man stands on the table.

"Your indulgence, fellow thespians!"

This got a loud response of laughter.

"If you could kindly take your drinks to the back, the first contest is in fifteen minutes."

The crowd slowly mingles its ways through to a large outhouse adjacent to the pub. Jess is feeling uncomfortable, but Sam reassures him, telling him he will do all the talking.

The first fight is about to begin, Sam looks around at the entourage, they are all tense, money is changing hands fast and furious, a bell rings, the two Staffordshire-bull terriers are let of their leashes from opposite corners, Jess looks to Sam, turns his head away, after thirty seconds, the saw-dust is thrown in the ten foot square, up in the air, on reaching the floor, it is mingled with the blood of the ferocious wounds now being opened by the teeth and nails of the dogs, the owners, when the dogs retreat, are further goaded forward to carry on their grizzly combat, above the abusive enthusiasm of the crowd a group of people are arguing about betting money, seconds later, a brawl erupts, the wounded dogs are taken out of the ring handlers, Sam makes a decision.

"Jess, take the dog, get in touch with McDonald tell him what's happened, I'll see you in the morning now go before you get arrested, if....."

"You sure? Will you be alright?"

"Don't worry, now scarper"

The fight had now taken over the whole meeting, dogs were running about barking, biting legs in their panic, as if getting their own back, it was bedlam, Sam stayed back as much as he could, but was a likely target, in a few seconds a bottle comes flying by, his head, he ducks the assailant comes towards him screaming in familiar way, Sam stands his ground, just about as he goes to grab Sam, he slips on the wet blooded sawdust, to help him on his way Sam hits him over the head with his "black jack" which was hidden up his sleeve, the fight had now spilled into the bar, just as he was about to leg it, he spots three men, punching, kicking a man up against the bar, pausing, gallantry his training takes over, running to help the victim the "black jack" made short work of two of them, the third made his escape, from behind both his arms were held, he saw a large knife about to stab him in the reflection of the mirror, he was helpless

"No no no!!! Leave him out, he fucking saved my beef"

The holder of the knife pauses, they release their grip

"What's your name mate?.... never mind come along with us, the ol' bill will be 'ere in a minute, don't wanna spend the night in a slammer

The henchmen pick up Albert, frog march him to the exit, above the melee, police whistles, racing to the scene dwindle out, as they get in to a large American car.

"That was a nice rescue.... what's your name?"

"Joe Fellows"

"Joe Fellows? Well Joe I gotta thank you for that, and I owe yuh! Porky, give the man one of our cards, ring me up later in the week, shame, that was the beginnings of a good night – what happened to your dog and his handler?"

"Yuh he scarpered with him, we got too much money invested in him, didn't wanna lose him if the old bill confiscated the dog, there'll be other nights"

"Sure there will, …..where d'you want dropping off?"

"Down on the corner of "The Cut" suit me fine"

On arrival at "The Cut" Sam alights from the car starts to walk through a courtyard to The Peabody building, he realises the car has not pulled away so he walks in the shadows, waits a few minutes, later the car slowly glides passed him, he smiles knowing the gang weren't quite sure of the new face on the block.

Next morning at 7am McDonalds office, George, Sam, are sitting around a table facing McDonald

"So how'd it go? The pub smashed up, we're the new owners of eight made-for fighting mad dogs and you're smiling"

"It ain't as bad as it seems!"

"Well come on, surprise me"

"You said to me an George get as much info as you can about the gang and its connections, well far short of sitting 'em down and asking them questions over a brown all I got the next best thing....." He pauses for dramatic effect.

"Well?"

"Albert, they call him "Face" have me card to phone him in the week, which I thought you might be please about"

McDonald nods his head

"That's good work, right, from now on you two will have to go under cover, any info goes straight to me in this office, no dialogue to any of your mates"

"The only thing I found a bit dicky, why was the fight started? You would have though all that planning, money involved an' that"

McDonald smirks "Yuh I heard it was a riot, my pikey pals like the little skirmish, especially when their getting paid for it."

Sam and George look at one another smiles.

Two days later Rose, with two friends of the gang pull up outside "Whitelys" in Queensway, once inside they casually wonder through the store not speaking, the trio, look at the different displays, nod their heads 'no', walk through to the escalator to alight at the first floor, wondering around not creating any attention to themselves, they review several shop windows until they stop at ones which particularly interest them, look at one another nod their heads in recognition of the spoils to be had, walking nonchalantly past, they go over to the opposite side of the store, turn after several stops, then cross back over, they enter the shop they had targeted, the two sales assistants greet them with a courteous smiles at the same time eyeing up the well healed characters

"Good morning, how may I help you?"

"I would like to see that little dress you have in the window display, it looks quite continental?"

"Yes madam is right, it's French"

The other gang members got to different corners of the store, one sits down while the other one slowly looks through the racks of dresses, takes one out to put against her body, Rose is watching to see when the time was right to put their well rehearsed plan into action, while the gang member sitting down, nods to her colleague

"Could I try this one on?"

"Certainly madam, the changing room is adjacent at the end of the rack"

Rose is passing by with her dress

"Could I possibly see it in the light, ifs for a garden party?"

"Absolutely, perhaps madam could take it outside"
"Splendid"

They both walk out

Colleague No 2 have now got the attention of the sales assistant, helping her to choose her dress, colleague number three quickly looks around to take advantage of the security lapse, getting up she turns to a dress rail behind, quickly, professionally, slides three dresses quickly folds them, puts them in her cummerbund, squeezes them as hard as she can.

Rose with perennial vision looks through the shop front window to see the operation successful, slowly saunters back in the shop where the colleagues slowly move to make their exit, the junior sales assistant being courteous to her customer, takes the dress to put it back on the hanger.

"If the garment doesn't interest madam we do have some new stock arriving from Paris at the end of the week – perhaps madam would like to re-visit us?"

"That would be admirable, thank you"

Rose enters the shop, followed by the owner

"It's a shame but what I was after was a garment that would show up its ambience at late night garden party, never mind, are you ready girls?"

"Yes Rose"

The trio slowly walk to the door, the young sales assistant calls out, the trio look at one another their faces harden, one of them tightens the grip on her umbrella.

"Would madam like to take our business card, when you come again we will arrange a discount"

"Thank you so much"

They leave the shop they had taken several steps when a male voice behind orders them to stop, they turn quickly.

"Bloody building security, right take a different path to the car," following a well know withdrawal plan, the trio run in different directions, to different exits, staircases, the security man hesitates, this was to be his downfall, it gave two girls valuable time to mingle in to the customers parading in the store, the security man loses sight of Rose, he beams on to her still several seconds in front of him, she side-steps in another dress shop, a window dressers is re-dressing some nude mannequins, Rose stands by one of them, motionless, the pursuer stops by the window, he is perplexed to where she had disappeared too, he casually looks around then looks full forward to the nude mannequins, staring at them, the window dresses turns, the man is embarrassed she waves her arm for him to go, he does, the window dresser turns to Rose

"You know you get all sorts here, bloody pervert, still I supposed it made his day, can I help you madam?"

"No, I can see your busy, I'll come back another day to see your mannequins fully clothed without the fear of being gawked at."

They both laugh

The other two girls by way of going down different stairs stand apart from one another concealing themselves in doorways across the road, waiting for Rose to appear, Rose waits for the pursuer to go to the ladies toilet where he waits for several minutes, this is what Rose was waiting for, it signalled her departure, walking briskly she studies the exits to the main road, the girls run across as she starts up the car, jumping in laughing, Rose turns the car round just as the security man appears out on to the main entrance, scouring both ways for the girls, as they pass, they put their heads down

"That was pretty close Rose"

"Yuh, good training though, keeps us on our toes, so what did we borrow?"

The girl with the muff so reels out her gains to expose the dresses, laying them across her and the other girls lap, Rose look through her mirror.

"Hold them up, very nice bit of schmutter, Alice should be well pleased"

They start to sing.

Two days later Sam is walking down Blackfriars Road towards the "Elephant and Castle", a large American car pulls up just in front of him, a door opens a voice beckons him in,

"Jump in Joe"

Once inside he looks around at his company, it was the same men who dropped him off the night of the fight

"Albert wants to show his appreciation for the rumpus caused a couple of days ago, he was a bit sorry he didn't see your dogs fight, so to make it up to you, he suggested that you be his guest at another fight, but this time with two legs instead of four"

The others start to laugh. After travelling for another ten minutes they stop at a pub on the corner of "The Cut" . Sam is a bit apprehensive,

"Don't worry, you should enjoy this, follow me"

The entourage walk through the public bar through to a door, it leads to a large hall, the prominent fixture being a boxing ring in the centre, enclosed with six rows of seats on each side. It was silent, Sam looks around, they gesture him to walk down to the front row, he looks at the ring, it has a short sprinkling of saw-dust, two corner men in each corner look up from administrating the water, towels, nod in recognition.

One of the group gestures Sam to sit down, dispelling any thought of walking away, the individual places a firm hand on his arm, smiles, Sam slowly sits down, a space is left on his right.

"Drink?"

"Yuh I'll have brown ale"

"No this is a special occasion, have a spirit or champagne"

"Okay gin and make it a double"

"That's better, now you're talking"

From behind Sam hears the talking of people coming to take their places in a few minutes the hall is filled, then the applause starts, from opposite sides of the ring, two of the largest men Sam had ever seen, slowly climb up the treads to enter the ring. A hand puts a glass in front of Sam.

"See what I mean – two legs."

The group laugh, the combatant men rub their boots into the saw dust, the referee gets into the ring, looks over to Sam's party, the leader nods his head "no", two minutes later there is a loud road, clapping, whistling, Sam looks around, Albert is walking down the gangway, slowly raises his hand to acknowledge the crowd, he comes to sit next to the vacant chair adjacent to Sam. The master of ceremonies looks over, Albert nods his head.

"Gentlemen, could we have a bit of hush for the first bout of the evening; firstly though I would like to introduce our patron, please be upstanding for Mr Albert Ross, who, though he's most generous donation to our local charities, has endeavoured to make the Borough of Southwark a much more pleasant place to live, especially for our children......"

The whole place erupted, everybody standing up clapping, whistling, chanting Albert's name, he gets up waving his arms gesticulating to the crowd, Sam looks around in disbelief as he slowly gets up, Albert sits down.

"You didn't have to get up, you're my guest......"

"Now to business, this is a twelve-round contest between and introducing my right corner, weighing in at fifteen stone from Plaistow, would you give a South London welcome to Bomber Holder"

The crowd show their appreciation by cheering and booing, he looks around scowling at the unappreciated reception.

"In my left corner all the way from North London, Dave the "Slayer" Rogers... weighing in at sixteen stone...."

The crowd once again show their appreciation in the same manner. The M/C leaves the ring, the referee beckons that two combatants to touch gloves, the "Slayer" goes to touch gloves but stops midway to throw a punch knocking his opponent back to the ropes, the crowd roar their approval, with booing whistling, the referee gets in between the two, The Slayer strides over, they are in a clinch, he uses his forehead to nut "Bomber" across his nose, more baying from the crowd referee pushes "The Slayer" back, he goes to a neutral corner, the referee starts his count, it goes beyond ten, "Bomber" shakes his head to carry the fight to this opponent. It was to be a foretaste of the bloody rounds to come.

At the end of the third, both boxers faces are blooded, eyes half closed, whelp marks over their torsos, the crowd baying for more punishment. By this time Sam is a bit perplexed, bracing himself not to show ignorance of the sport he turns to his left to speak to one of the gang.

"What's going on? He's hitting him with rabbit punches, butted each other, gouged their eyes, long counts, Jesus what is this?"

The other men in the adjacent seats all smile, then start to laugh.

"Listen Joe I gotta explain, they don't fight under the "Queensbury" rules 'ere, it called unlicensed boxing, and mostly anything goes, well mostly anything, they don't stand for kicking in the balls …"

"Your joking in'chyuh, I've seen that as well"

A voice chirps up, they laugh

"Anyway you've noticed the cuts an' all that, their gloves are under the proper weight, really you could say it's like bar-knuckle fighting like in the ol' days, see"

Joe nods his head, frowning at the expose. By the end of the eighth round both boxers face, torsos' were covered in blood, bruises and whelps in the last ten seconds, "Bomber" was pulled away from a clinch, The "Slayer" saw his chance, instead of taking a step back he went forward to hit him with a right upper cut, followed by a haystack left-hand, "Bomber" fell to the canvas in a heap; pandemonium broke out, everybody to a man stood up, clapping, booing, yelling, whistling, noggins, were first thrown into the ring, after this show of gratitude, the real feelings of the crowd showed their real colours, the loose chairs were thrown into ring, bottles, glasses, anything miscellaneous, the referee tried to protect the fighters but he succumb to the barrage, after being hit by a chair, self preservation took over, he awkwardly climbed through the ropes holding a towel over an open wound on his head.

Sam looked on in desperation as the missiles flew over his head, his associates on both sides of him, pulled their jackets over their heads, laughing joining in the melee, and chaos going on, slowly the disturbance died down, the stewards got into the ring, trying to protect the embattled boxers, the time keeper rattled his bell, this caused the audience to settle down. A steward gets into the ring, and through his hand-held microphone called for order.

"Gentlemen can I have your attention? Due to technical knockout, the referee, judges have declared "The Slayer" the winner, please show your appreciation for a brave and gallant looser....."

This led to more whistling, heckling as the "Bomber" was helped through the ropes by his seconds "The Slayer" pompously walked round the ring, nodding his head to the baying crowd.

"Well Joe what d'you think of our ladies night? It's a shame, still I earned a couple of ponies right lads let's get out of 'ere before the bleeding place erupts into a volcano"

They pick their way through the audience, just as they get to the pub door, a fights going on between two men, trying to get passed one of them mistakenly throws a punch at Albert, just as he is about to connect he notices who it is, starts to withdraw the threat,

"Sorry Albert!"

But it was too late, Albert's bodyguards jump on the victim, kicking him, pummelling him to the ground, leaving him in a crumpled heap, Joe looks at the victim.

"Don't worry Joe, he'll be alright in the morning"

"Well Joe, how do y'like your first introduction of the pugilistic sport?"

"Well I don't think it's something I could recommend"

"That's fair enough, horses for courses"

They are now sitting around a table drinking

"Well Joe I suppose our last couple of get togethers' wasn't particularly for the feint hearted and it don't show much decorum an don't represent our true image, but to show you the other side of our life style...."

One of his gang interrupts

"We run a school of ballroom dancing, down at the Trocadera, down at the Elephant Tuesday afternoons........"

Another of the group intervene,

"Yuh don't be late, we have tea, cakes brought round, the best time is the "Excuse me", all the favourite songs "Al Bowly, Joe has you'd love it"

"That's enough – Joe, we having a party Saturday night a little celebration like, I'd like you to cone."

"Much appreciated, can I bring a pal?"

"Course yuh can – you'll enjoy it, plenty of drink, entertainment, girls"

"Right that'll do me"

The next morning Joe is talking to James McDonald in a coffee shop in Soho. "George these people live in a different world, they throw money around as if there was no tomorrow"

"I know don't worry, we gotta play along until we got a east-iron case against them, they gave a couple of beaks in their pocket an some chief inspector down at the yard, I've been on this case for nearly two years, I don't wanna blow it through lack of incompetence of my superiors...... now when you go to this party, you an' George make a mental note of all the main faces, don't drink too much, get both of your stories well rehearsed, most important of all make sure you can back 'em up make no mistake they'll play you along just to make sure who you are, don't be clever and try to mug 'em off"

"Right"

"I'll make arrangements to meet you at the Hyde Park speakers corner, you can give me all the names you can remember, we'll mingle with the punters, then go our separate ways."

Sam nods his head.

FRIDAY MORNING

Rose, tow of her friends are in Knightsbridge, walking passed Derry & Toms they look at the display in the windows, then casually walk in, they cause no suspicion as they walk through to the gift section of the store, spreading their way along a covered counter the Rose, asks the assistant to look at a collection of paper weights, the distraction had been begun, whilst Rose queries the make, origin of the species, the other two girls engage themselves at the far ends of each counter, Rose is pointing at some flaws in the pieces, the assistant bends down to have a look at the problem, this was their chance, the two girls made their move, putting their bags and brollies on the table, to cover a display of high value pens, on the other end, the girl purposely drops down, then reaches behind the counter to scoop up a tray of imitation rings, they both walk away in opposite directions. Rose thanks the sales assistant but it wasn't quite what she was looking for.

On to the second floor the trio meet up in the cafeteria, indulging in tea, pastries, seemingly well pleased with three minute shoplifting.

"Christ hang on, I think we've been fingered"

From across the room a large man strides towards their table, they all look at one another pensively, there was nowhere to run. They all put their hands to their hats ready to retrieve the hat pins

"Excuse me ladies, did you just visit the gift counter downstairs?"

One of the girls slowly raises her hand to lace it on the large hat pin, ready to stab the man in the face,

"Yes"

"Oh good, I believe you must have dropped this item from your purse...."

He hands one of the girls a small silver cross.

"That's very kind of you, thank you"

"My pleasure madam, compliments of the store"

She pushes back the hat pin. The girls quickly drink their tea waiting for the store detective to exit.

"Right girls lets disappear while we're in front!"

Chapter 3

SATURDAY NIGHT: A RESTAURANT IN DRURY LANE

The atmosphere is heavy, music in the background, Joe, George Ross, Albert, Alice Diamond, her entourage, and Rose, are all seated around a large round table, Alice is eyeing up the group, slowly focusing on Joe, George, she asks in Albert's ear "Who are these new faces?" Albert explains the situation, then from behind the m/c announces the next dance will be a slow fox trot.

"D'you know I've often wondered if the bloke who invented the fox trot, seen a fox trot, you know what I mean, did he go up to it and say I can dance like that?"

They all laugh. Rose catches Joe's eyes, looks away

"Joe would you like to dance with Rose?"

"I would be delighted"

Once on the dance floor, Rose started the conversation.

"I hear Albert got a soft spot for you after that fiasco up the pub, take it from me, keep in his good books, don't whatever you do try to be too clever or try to cross him"

"Rose, may I call you Rose? I wouldn't dream of it, stand on me."

As they walk back to the table Rose compliments him on his dancing. One of the group chirps up

"We'll have to call him Mr Twinkle Toes then"

As the party were well into their drinking session this went down well. Through the evening Joe at short intervals keeps looking in Rose's direction, she did not respond at first, so Joe gave up and distractedly took more notice of the session singers, making his excuses Joe decided it was time to go.

Albert was having none of it.

"Not yet Joe, they're just about to have a Tombola. Relax sit down"

Joe didn't need to be told twice.

The m/c interrupts the proceedings

"Ladies and gentlemen we've come to that time of the evening when we conduct our charity period, now we have some nice schmutter of cabbage which has been kindly donated by our patron Albert, and Alice, whom you all know and respect...."

A round of applause, a table is brought out with a collection of clothes, several dresses, a fur-coast, a box of other goodies were put under the table.

"Okay what am I bid for their designer dresses, brand new acquired from Selfridges?"

There is a large round of clapping, laughter, whistling "Five guineas, ten guineas, fifteen guineas, twenty guineas, a pause from the back of restaurant, a voice shouts out

"Thirty guineas!"

"Well done sir, she won't give you the old cold back tonight"

Applause, all the items that went up for auction were the items that had been stolen from their shop lifting exercise earlier on that week

"And now ladies and gentlemen for something quite different, and to boost our charity money, we would like the ladies to donate anything they decide could be of any worth, if they would like to bring their male companion up with them to protect them, that would be most appreciated."

There is a pause all round the restaurant, women start to look at their fingers. Grudgingly take off a ring, slowly they walk onto the dance floor to form a line, Alice looks across to Rose, nods her head in the direction of Joe, she nods back "yes"

"Joe would you mind accompanying me to the floor"

Joe is taken aback; Rose leaves her bag, Joe wondering what she has to offer. There are now eight attractive women on the line, the first one offers the m/c a fox fur stole.

"Ladies, gentleman what am I to offer for this beautiful stole, it would gladden the heart of any lady to go to the ball?"

Applause, the offer goes up to forty guineas.

The next women offers a ring, this hot a sixty guinea price tag. Now it was Rose's turn, she has a word in his ear. "Now something special; tonight and for one night only Rose is going to treat us, dim the lights and put the spotlight on Rose."

Joe stands to the side, Rose, very slowly starts to lift her dress which has a split in the side then stops.

"Twenty quid" she lifts it a little big higher "Thirty quid", a little bit higher "forty guineas" - the atmosphere is quiet, tense, "sixty quid", a little higher they went on pass, more shouts at it got to the top of her thigh which exposed a bright red garter.

"Well my friends that's enough excitement for one night – what am I to bid for the garter?"

"A century" Albert looks round gets up, quietly beckons over the m/c

"Albert has more generously offered one-hundred and fifty pounds"

A pause, the restaurant is silent

"Albert the garter is yours"

Rose slowly slides the garter down her leg, throws it to Albert, catches it, slides it over his cigar, the restaurant erupts

On their way back to their seats Joe quietly speaks.

"That was a turn up for the books you took my breath away"

Rose squeezes his hand laughs; they sit down, Alice taps her glass, the table goes quiet.

"I would just like to congratulate Albert on what a wonderful evening we have all had and if this is the way that we are going to carry on, our partnership can only flourish."

The group taps the table in response, Albert waits for the gratification to die down, raises his hand, and stands up with the cigar still on his mouth, the group laugh.

"Firstly it's been a wonderful evening, the auction, gifts, have been well received, the donation will make a welcome donation to our charities in Southwark, secondly I would like to honour Rose in doing the right thing to getting people in the right mood for the auction, raise your glasses, but I would like to see the other garter, just for old time's sake"

The group show their appreciation.

"How are you going to get home Rose?"

Joe asks

"Not to worry, on do's like these Albert lays on the works, he's got a couple of limo's to take us all home...."

"Can I travel with you?"

"We'll have to see how it works out, Alice is a bit quirky about mixing business with pleasure"

They all slowly got up to leave, Joe takes the hint, lags behind so that he looks inconspicuous moving out to the foyer. Rose looks round, smiles but she is ushered into the first car, which is quickly filled up, pulls away, leaving Joe to get into the second car.

The next Sunday Sam is making his way to Hyde Park, speakers corner, making sure he is not being followed he changes buses twice, then gets off at the middle of Park Lane, walking the rest of the way to the meeting. They had decided earlier to meet at a coffee stall, adjacent to the railings, both taking different stances at the coffee stall, avoiding each other, Sam finishes his coffee, walks casually to mingle two or three deep in the throng, McDonald finishes his coffee walks in the opposite direction manoeuvring himself until he is adjacent to Sam.

"Bloody hell you couldn't have picked a better meet, guv!"

"Yuh I know, I didn't want to blow your cover for the sake of a bit of forethought, right enough of the niceties tell me names, times and anything miscellaneous, keep it short to the point."

In three minutes Sam still looking ahead, informed Foden of the night's meeting. Satisfied, McDonald turns in the opposite direction just as the crowd had picked up on a heated discussion, shouting, raising their hands, showing their approval or disapproval, it was a perfect way to end their clandestine meeting. Sam waiting several minutes then made his departure in the opposite direction.

Monday: Alice is in the parlour of her house, laid out on a large table, she is sifting through several days of stolen goods, the small value items were placed in cardboard boxes. Rose was on the opposite side of the table, taking in every move Alice was making.

"You watching me my girl, take everything in, you could maybe be in this position one day"

For fifteen minutes she meticulously filtered out the small value items, then with a slight of her hand, puts a valuable piece of jewellery in the box, pushes it over to Rose.

"Right what do you think of that little gang, go on 'ave a shifty, tell me what you think"

Rose, slowly, intently goes through the hoard, picking up individual pieces, looking at them at all different angles, picks up the valuable items looks at it, sensing something different, puts it to one side, Alice notices straight away, pauses.

"Good girl, no need to look any further you found the nice piece, those pieces we'll take down East Street, an' punt 'em out to some of my market friends, now this pieces are obviously of higher quality, we'll take to the pawn-brokers, and jewellery shops, that way everybody's happy, no loose ends – What'd think Rose? Good business?" Rose smiles.

"Alice I think you're in the wrong business you should be in, I dunno, banking, organising things, you know like being a buyer for shops an' the like..."

They both look at one another realising what Rose had said, they both burst out laughing.

"Are you sure? Me a buyer, yuh, it would be coming in one door 'n' going out the other, the bleeding store would be bankrupt in a week"

They both carry on laughing, start to drink.

At the end of the table is a neat pile of the dresses they had shoplifted over the past week.

"Now with these nice little numbers we'll pack 'em up an' go for a little ride that will interest you"

Getting out of a taxi in Petticoat lane, the man-handle their large carpet bags in to a millinery, haberdashery shop, the owner from behind the counter greets Alice with a smile and a nod. A young assistant is counting out some buttons adjacent.

"Sophie, would you kindly help this lady in choosing a colour match to go with the dress?"

Turns to Alice, in a raised voice

"Would you like to follow me into the workroom I can give you back your samples"

Entering the room two middle ladies are seated at a table with a dress each, Alice walks over, beckoning Rose – smiles and looks down.

"That's what you call a work of art."

Rose scrutinises what they're doing, looking above their small glasses, they are carefully unpicking the manufacturers labels from a small box, one of the seamstresses is sewing a new label with different cotton, finishing it, she hands it to Rose, looking at the finished item in awe

"Amazing"

The lady smiles

"Well it beats working back-stage at Drury Lane an' pays a lot better don't it girls?"

They acknowledge Alice with a nod, and a smile still concentrating on the job.

"Come over here Alice, put your bags on the table, it's been a good earner that last cotchal you brought in......"

From a small money box she unlocks and retrieves a round bundle of elasticized notes – Alice puts it in her bag.

"Stop for a nice cup of tea, look at this"

She picks up a finished dress, puts it up against Rose

"This'll be sold to the pretty things; Knightsbridge, Chelsea, Mayfair, who knows?"

They sit down to their tea.

That afternoon at Georges pub, he is holding court, around the table the table are his enforceable lieutenants, they are slowly drinking their beers.

"You know George I got a funny feeling about the "Forty Thieves", what I mean is, they seem to be well organised, everything they attempt they get away with like: Alice must have a mind of a bleeding field commander...."

"What d'you know about field commanders? Just because you couldn't organise a piss-up in a brewery it don't mean there ain't clever birds out there!"

They all chuckle; George waits for the laughter to die down

"You both right, but as far as I can see they ain't doing a bad job, all we do is supply the muscle, the getaway cars, take a percentage of the proceeds, I reckon we should carry on, we don't get our fingers dirty, 'ole bill leaves us alone, what more d'you want?"

"Well we could advertise for a Field Marshall"

Laughter.

TWO DAYS LATER

Sam is walking down Berwick Street W.I Ending up to go in to a speak easy, he finds an empty booth, after a short interval a hostess appears asking for his order

"Two large gins"

Coming from the opposite direction Foden saunters in the club, looks round then casually walks over to Sam's booth.

"Got anything for me?"

"Well I've been invited to another bash this weekend....."

The hostess brings the order over.

"It seems their liaison is bearing fruit, I might be able to get an "in" with Alice by way of one of her young protégés..."

"Listen, don't go in too quick, let this bird do all the talking, you do all the listening, don't come on to her too quick, you know what I mean, just nibble at the cake, the chief has given us cart blanche on the time factor, he just wants this thing cut 'n' dry no loose ends, by the way how's George shaping up?"

"He's a good kid, know when to keep his mouth shut, don't ask any questions, how's the crew, they getting inquisitive about our absence?"

"Yuh, but I told them you've gone on a government training course for the MI5, there all gonna have a turn so they don't ask any questions"

Foden finishes his dink

"Don't push the expenses too much, you know what I mean, phone me next week"

He leaves, Sam gives him ten minutes, then leaves by the fire exit.

A day later, Leather Lane market on East Street market

Alice is casually walking down the middle of the market, the stalls on either side, Alice stops to buy some fruit

"You know what they say Rose, an apple a day keeps the ol' bill away"

Once paying for the fruit, Alice goes up to a stall which has jewellery laid out in purple baize glass covered boxes, she catches the eye of the vendor. He nods, looks casually at both ends of the market, he bends down to pick up a large empty display cabinet, placing it exactly over one of the boxes on the stall, Alice from her large carpet bag, puts a handful of imitation jewellery onto the baize, she lowers her other hand to pull Rose gently to her side to cover the transaction, the vendor sifts through the items, spreading them apart to appraise the items.

"Thirty quid"

"Forty"

"Meet me half way, Twenty Five"

"Thirty"

"Done"

The vendor covers the tray puts down under his stall, slipping the money to her, they stay for a few minutes, walk away, Alice offers Rose an apple, looking down at the bag, the money is inside.

"Look an' learn Rose, if we were to get our collars felt, I'd just drop the bag on the floor, no evidence, no prisoners"

At the end of the market they make a detour into Hatton Garden, slowly looking in different windows, crossing the road, all the time Alice nonchalantly looking to see if they are being followed, satisfied crossing back over, they look at two more jewellery shops until they come to a pawn brokers, casually looking at the display, they enter.

A bespectacled Jewish man is looking at a watch with a customer; putting down his eye glass he offers the man a valuation.

"Fifty pounds – to be redeemed in two weeks"

"Is that all? It is a genuine Patek Phillipe, it's an heirloom"

"I know, but that's the best I can do"

He catches the eye of Alice, gets a bit agitated, the punter nods yes.

"If you'd like to go over to the cashier he'll give you your receipt, thank you"

"Hello Alice nice to see you"

"Likewise"

"Would you like to come out the back, have a little chaser?"

They follow him through to a small parlour, once the two are seated, he locks the door, then peeps through a small hole.

"Never can be too careful Alice, so who is this nice young lady? We haven't met before"

"That's right"

"Lovely Alice, always the soul of discretion, we'll show me what's in your Pandora's Box"

Alice unbuttons her coat, revealing the large pockets from which she extrudes a black bag, slowly empties the contents on the table.

The man's eyes light up, he moves the items so they are individually separate.

"You've done yourself proud this time Alice"

Putting his eye glass to his eyes, he appraises the item, putting the last piece down.

"Well Alice...... £250"

"I was thinking more along the lines of £350"

He picks up his eye glass again, looks at the merchandise again, pauses, "£275"

"As its Easter £300"

He nods his head smiles,

"You're in the wrong religion, you should be called Linda"

"And you should be called Dick Turpin"

They both laugh. "It's a deal, we'll celebrate the deal with a nice glass of wine"

Alice inadvertently displays her hand on the table, Albie goes to hand her the glass, but is transfixed by Alice's hand, each finger has gold, silver rings, but mostly diamond rings on each of her fingers, he puts down the glass adjacent to her hand.

"Spread your hand for me Alice"

Gets his eye glass to inspect them,

"These are absolute perfection, where did you acquire them?"

"All part of the game Albie, do you want to look at my other hand?"

She places both her hands on the table, Albie is near salivating over the spectacle, looking up, straight into her eye,

"You must have over ten thousand pounds worth of jewellery on your hands, did you know that?"

"Not really, it's just a collection I acquired over the years, you could call it my insurance really, some people put their money in the bank, I'd rather keep my collateral where I can see it"

"I believe I can now call you Diamond Annie"

"You can call me what you bloody want as long as you fence my goods at a top price"

"Now let's drink to that Annie"

Alice puts on her gloves to hide her rings. Leaving the shop after conducting her business Annie is in a good mood.

"Right Rose, with you cabbage you've got in your bag we'll visit our last port-of-call, we're going into Indian Country: d'yuh know Islington? Well it can be a bit tasty, but if we do our business quick we should be alright, let's get a cab"

Pulling up outside a terrace house Alice knocks on a sliding panel which is pulled back, then closed, the door opens

"Alice long time no see, come in"

A middle aged women leads them into a large room, there are a collection of men, women drinking, Alice has made sure she has her gloves on.

"Alice you might know some of my friends"

Alice looks around nods her head, slowly putting her hand to her hat making sure the hat pin is protruding long enough if she is to use it in an emergency.

"Come through to the back>"

Rose follows, eyeing up the gathering.

"Right, what you got for me?"

Rose places her bag on the table, taking out all the lingerie, trinkets, pens. The women eye up the spoils spreading them into different piles.

"You've got some nice items here Annie"

She holds up a pair of bras, then some underwear

"Someone's going to be lucky tonight"

They laugh, the woman pauses

"Fifty pounds Alice"

"Done"

From outside a voice calls

"What you doing in there?"

"Just coming – Annie you got time for quick snort?"

"No thanks, we're in a bit of a rush"

The woman hands her the money, as they walk through the adjoining room, Rose notices the white powder on several of the tables, women in a daze on long settees, men drooling over them, after closing the door, Annie starts to walk quick, hailing a cab

"Bloody glad to get away from her, don't let me catch you going down that road young lady"

That night at Alice's house, all the gang are gathered, the atmosphere is heavy with cigarette smoke, everybody has a drink in their hand.

"Right girls, lets come to order get round the table, make yourself comfortable." Rose is sitting adjacent to her.

"We've had a good month, no one's had their collar felt so, as they say "there's pickings for all""

The girls whistle, clap.

"Right, Rose will hand out all the envelopes, I haven't bothered to put your names on 'em 'cos you've all got the same"

From a medium sized money box, Rose hands out the envelopes, they are passed around the table until all of the girls have one, it goes quiet for a few seconds, then the pandemonium starts up again, as they count the contents, they all make a bee line to Alice to embrace her, Alice gets embarrassed.

"That's enough, I see that I'll have to cut back on your wages if I get any more of this."

Two days later Foden, Sam are on the rails at Walthamstow dog track, they are separated by two bookie stands, after two races, Foden goes to the bookie to lay his bet, Sam waits for him to wonder off and mingle in the opposite direction, Sam goes up to the same bookie lays his bet, gets his ticket

Foden goes up to the Tote lays his bet, Sam goes to the adjacent window, lays his bet, pockets his ticket

Sam is at the bar, casually gets out his tickets, casually looks at it, the next race is about to start. At the finish, Sam hears over the tannoy his dog has lost, making a point, of shaking his head, he looks at his ticket, it has a message on it, "Ring me A.S.A.P" tears it up in very small pieces, drops it on the floor, rubs his shoes into the remains, kicks it away, finishes his beer, exits.

Next morning: he rings Foden.

"Everything going alright Sam?"

"Yuh, cushty"

"Right I want you to up the stakes, how d'you think you're fixed with Rose, can you push it to ask her out?"

"I dunno, she was all over me like a rash at the restaurant, could have been the booze talking....."

"Well that's the chance we gotta take, you get in touch with her, take her out, try to find their next escapade....."

"Hang on Jim, she ain't no walkover, she's a very astute bird, plus if they get an inkling that I'm being pushy it'll jeopardise everything and I'll end up in the sausage factory"

"Do your best"

Two days later, late morning, Alice, Albert are in a pub drinking. Alongside Albert is a bookkeeper taking down notes in a ledger as they confer.

"Well Alice it looks like our enterprise has proved lucrative, we set up a nice chain of fences, got a few coppers weighed in, I'm satisfied.... I got another proposition to put to you..."

"Albert, one thing at a time, my girls are earning well, I admit that, but I want to lay them off for a bit, their getting a bit exhausted, all the running about 'n' everything, not to mention a few near misses, Alice Turner got three months, Maggie Hughes got caught running out of a jewellers with a tray of thirty four diamond rings, the worst part of it was she ran right into the arms of a copper."

Albert smiles "Alice I know it ain't funny, but did she drop the tray?"

Alice shakes her head, she is not amused

"Okay, down to business, a lot of your girls are attractive, and pretty, right? Well what I was thinking of – I dunno how you're going to take this, but how about a bit of blackmail?"

"No, no, no, my girls could go down for a long stretch if they get collared."

"Listen to me, I would pick the most vulnerable geysers, just a little bit of seducing, nothing too complicated, get a payment, and walk away, what could be easier? My minder would be in the background all the time, everybody gets paid, a nice little enterprise."

"I'll put it to my girls, maybe they might be interested."

"Okay you've finished with the ledger-work, give Alice her wedge, then drinks all round"

"Albert I want a quiet word, let's go over to the corner: the old bill might be getting a bit close, we had a close shave the other week as you know, we go into one large store do the business, hopefully get away, right, what I propose is we raid a collection of shops across the West End of the city simultaneously, now once the ol' bill get the alarm, which one will they go to? They don't have the resources to focus on more than one store, by the time they sort themselves out, we've been 'n; gone, what'd you think?"

Albert takes a long drag on his cigar, blows the smoke over Alice's head, nodding his head for several seconds, he points his finger moving it up and down.

"What do I think? What do I bloody think? It's unbelievable, the simplest ideas are always the best, have you got enough girls? I can organise the getaways, I'll use my best drivers, yuh' I like it Alice, you work out the finer details, cross the "T"s, dot the "I"s, luv it, do you know Alice, you should have been a prime minister in the war, it would have ended two years earlier"

They both laugh

"Yuh I would have look right dandy marching down "Black Friars Road" with all them medals on m'chest."

Next Day – Mid Morning: George and Sam are drinking at a coffee stall

"Well Sam have you heard anything on the grapevine? It appears Alice has been doing quite well over the last of months, recruiting new girls, teaching them the arts of shoplifting, you gotta hand it to her, she knows her business"

"Yuh I'll drink to that, can't take it away from her mind you, it just amazes me how she passes on an' keeps the loyalty of the girls"

"Well what you gotta look at is what would they be doing otherwise – in service, waiting hand 'n' foot on some old spinster or a randy retired Colonel, you can't blame 'em for getting out of the poverty"

Sam nods his head in agreement.

"The thing that fascinates me about all this, is the local people won't have a word said about em, the loyalty you can't put a price on, whenever our boys go round to question them, they all clam up, act schtum, we ain't got a chance of breaking up this little enterprise"

"Maybe, we'll have to work on it, I've spoken to Foden, he wants us to carry on the way we are, seems he's building up a nice little dossier"

"How you getting on with Rose – any naughties yet?"

"No I don't wanna push it, I'm taking her to the "Trocadera" tomorrow night, try to get her slowly tanked up, might weasel something out of her"

"Lucky you"

They finish their coffees, depart in different direction.

IN THE POLICE COMMANDERS OFFICE

Foden is seated opposite the commander

"Well how are you progressing with your two insiders"

The commissioner has taken a personal interest in the situation and I've got to fill him in on any progress that I have; you have, is that a number of his social friends are involved with the owners of the stores, they don't understand how a group of women can hold the stores to ransom."

"Well, firstly sir, they're not just a bunch of chancers, their well organised, led dare I say it, by a clever, well disciplined, ruthless women, by the name of Alice Diamond, her girls are very clever in what they do…"

"Nonsense, I get the feeling that you respect or indeed admire them, their felons, nothing more nothing less, so let's hear no more of this admire talk."

"I do admire them commander, because we don't have any arrests to speak of at the moment, they always seem to have a step in front, my two men have got into the inner circle and at this moment I am waiting on feedback from them"

"Well you best impress on them that I want some results before my next Masonic meeting, we have a ladies night coming up shortly, and I want to be the bearer of good news, that'll be all"

Foden leaves

Afternoon

Sam is waiting outside the Trocadero at the Elephant and Castle, Rose comes up behind him, taps him on the shoulder,

"Gotcha, been waiting long?"

"All of my life, you look ravishing, you got something you gotta tell me?"

"Like what?"

"Well have you had some good news, brought yourself something nice?"

"Both, I'll tell you about it all inside"

They are seated at the table for two, on the perimeter of the dance floor, music – people dancing

"Well what'd think of my new dress?"

She gets up, makes a complete slow turn

Sam is taken back of her beauty, he is open mouthed

"Well close your mouth, you'll be catching flies" she giggles

"You look breathtaking, that dress was inspired for you, if I never see you again I'll always remember how you look"

"Blimey don't go all romantic on me, you'll make me unhappy, now would you mind getting me some cigarettes off the usherette?"

"Will you still be here when I come back?"

"That's for me to know, you to find out, now fly and get my cigs"

On Sam's return Rose takes out a large cigarette holder from her bag, places the cigarettes in the holder, all the time looking in Sam's eyes, he is transfixed

"Any chance of a light young man? A girl could die of waiting"

Sam stretches his hand, lights the cigarette, there is a pause,

"Don't keep staring at me like that, people might think you like me"

He smiles.

After smoking the cigarette, they drink some tea

"Would you like to dance Sam? I'm getting itchy feet"

Once on the dance floor he holds her hesitantly, not wanting to get too close, she notices it, whispers in his ear.

"Get closer, I'm not going to bite you"

Sam increases his hold

"That's better much better, oh yes, the other thing I was going to tell you, I'm inviting you to a party next Saturday night, will you be my guest?"

"Just let anybody try an' stop me"

She giggles,

"Absolutely smashing"

Chapter 4

NEXT DAY BILLIARD HALL. CAMBRIDGE CIRCUS

Foden is at the opposite of the Hall, he walks over to a table which has just been vacated by two players, he places a half – a crown on the bulk-end of the table, Sam, George who are drinking walk over.

"Any takers?"

Foden asks

"Yuh, I take you on"

He places another half-a-crown next to the other one "My mate's hold the stake, I'll let you break"

Half way through the game the duo had not still not broken their silence, George brakes the stalemate by asking what drinks they want, they play on. By the time the game finishes Foden has won, George gives Foden the stake money.

"Wanna double or nothing?"

Foden ask

"Er no thanks, that's enough enjoyment"

"Any takers?"

Foden asks

"Yuh I'll take you on"

He places another half-a-crown next to the other one "My mate's hold the stake, I'll let you break"

Half way through the game the duo had still not broken their silence, George brakes the stalemate by asking what drinks they want, they play on. By the time the games finishes Foden has won, George gives Foden the stake money.

"Wanna double or nothing?"

Foden asks

"Er no thanks, that's enough enjoyment for one night, let's have a quickie at the bar!"

Foden makes a point of getting in between his two detectives, from the corner of his mouth, he asks if they have any news for him, looking in front, George replies

"We've been invited to a party on Saturday, I reckon my source has something big coming up, I'll meet you at London Zoo in the insect house, it's nice 'n' dark there, good cover"

"I bleeding 'ate spiders, you'd better have something good for me"

He finishes his drink walks away, the duo rack up for another game.

SATURDAY NIGHT, ANNIES HOUSE

The atmosphere in the large front room was going full strength, Sam, George were welcomed at the front door, leading to a passage, by a burly minder, who looks back to get a nod from an unseen guest they walk through to the front room, a pair of hands from behind Sam, covers his face.

"Guess who?"

"Mae West?"

"No, second guess?"

"Er Veronica Lake?"

"I'm leaving; I've never been so insulted in my short life"

Sam turns to face Rose, she looked splendid, dressed as a flapper girl, with a large boa round her neck, holding a large cigarette holder, she kisses Sam on the cheek, then George.

"You look stunning, something out of the pictures"

"I bet you say that to all your girls"

"No, only three of them"

They both laugh.

"Come over, I like to formally introduce to Alice, we didn't have much time at our last meeting"

He follows Rose through the melee, Alice is small talking to a group of girls.

"Alice I'd like to introduce you to Sam, he's my knight in shining armour, got two left feet though"

"I've heard a lot about you Sam, I hope you are not leading our best…."

She stops in mid sentence, not thinking what she was saying

"Erm, Seamstress"

"I can see that Alice, the way she's run up her dress"

Rose flirtingly pushes him

"Right, let's get you and George a drink"

She wanders off

"Well now it seems you've hit it off with Rose, what line of business are you in?"

Making sure he's got his cover story well rehearsed Sam answers her,

"Well me an' my mate George here, do a bit of buying 'n' selling down the Isle of Dogs, the docks, cigarettes, booze, perfume, y'know the odd luxuries of life"

"What about your leisure time?"

"A bit of dog fighting, over 'ackney marshes, anything with an angle, about you?"

"Well a bit like you really, but more on the feminine side:- Ah, here's Rose, right you be a good compere and look after our guests, don't want them going home without enjoying themselves"

"She's a really nice women..."

"Really nice but I wouldn't like to be in anybody's shoes if she's put out, drink up"

TWO HOURS LATER

Music is playing when it is turned down, the entourage look instinctively to the door, Albert walks in with his minder

"Evening all, don't stop for me"

A young lady walks up quickly to give him a drink, Alice makes her way over to him, they embrace,

"Nice mix Alice, good to see everybody's having a good time; can we go somewhere to have a little parley?"

They walk into a back room, Sam watches the manoeuvre, he is powerless to make any sudden move to follow them, as this would arouse instant suspicion, Rose comes back to Sam, and her hand clinches his down by his side.

"Hope your enjoying the atmosphere big boy,"

"Couldn't have wished for a better night, mind you not as good as bit of coursing"

"You peasant"

They both squeeze each other.

Inside the parlour, Albert's bodyguards gently ushers out three couples who have took up station, they leave with a murmur.

"Alice I've been thinking over your suggestion of hitting four stores at once, I can organise the man power, but do you have enough girls to coordinate the raids?"

"Don't worry about that side of it, all my girls are professionals, my main worry is the getaway they must be good drivers, no chancers, I look after my girls, their loyal"

"Sure I understand, no need to worry on that score"

"Good we can work out the finer details tomorrow, OK, let's go an' enjoy the party"

Alice comes out of the parlour makes a bee line to Rose

"Now I can see you young things are enjoying yourselves so I won't bother you no more tonight, Rose I'll see you ten o'clock tomorrow here, right as the host I've got to mingle"

TWO O'CLOCK IN THE MORNING

Sam, George are just finishing their drinks when Albert walks over

"You boys enjoying yourselves? Good, Sam can you drive?"

Sam nods

"I mean drive, like your life depended on it?"

"Yuh"

"Well I might have a nice little earner for yeh, I'll be in touch"

"Right"

Sam walks over to Rose kisses her on the cheek, he leaves with George.

A DAY LATER: INSIDE JOE LYONS ON THE STRAND

Foden is sitting at a table, Sam walks in casually sits on the next table with his back to Foden, picks up a newspaper, pauses.

"I've been invited to a meet with Albert, he wants to know if I can drive, I think something's occurring, would it be possible to get fast motor so that I have a bit of quick practice somewhere? Tune up my skills!"

"Bleeding 'ell who d'you think you are Raymond Navarro?"

"I'll arrange something sharpish, we got a place over the river, their building this airfield, I'll get clearance, keep in touch"

A waiter comes over to take Sam's order, Foden leaves.

EARLY MORNING: NEXT DAY: CROYDON AIRPORT

Sam is standing by a large American Buick car, listening intently to a driving instructor, once inside the car Sam slowly goes down the runway, the tarmac is wet owing to a dewy, misty morning, the instructor urges him to go forward, picking up speed, the car approaches a line of obstacles, the instructor puts his hand on the wheel to avoid them, the car starts to skid, the instructor yells to Sam to correct the slide, Sam does his best but cannot control the manoeuvre, hitting the obstacles, knocking them down like a bunch of skittles, the car carries on careering on the adjoining grass, a group of workers show their approval by cajoling, whistling, shouting good natured abuse. The procedure was started over again.

Throughout the day Sam was introduced to different kinds of manoeuvres, emergency stops, reversing at high speed, going round obstacles, controlling the car with flat tyres. The instructor finished late that night, Sam was mentally, physically drained. The next day the procedures were stepped up, he felt more confident as he honed the task. Once inside the small canteen they were seated, the instructor making rough sketches on paper, from behind a familiar voice broke up the pattern

"Well Sid how did our budding Navarro do?"

It was Foden

"He might be a threat if he carries on this way, well it was a crash course, but what can you do in two days?"

"Thanks Sid, right Sam let's have a little word in your shell like"

They walk over to a dimly lit corner.

"How was it left after the party?"

"I wasn't told anything specific, I'll have to bluff it through if he wants an experienced driver, I've got to ring him Friday night, see what the S.P. is, soon as I know anything I get to you"

"Right, just watch your back"

DAYTIME A PUB IN SOUTHAWK STREET.

A private room at the back, Rose, Albert and some gang members are seated around a table.

"Right Albert, I've decided on the stores. "Army & Navy", "Bourne and Hollingsworth", "Derry & Toms", and "Debenhams & Freebody".

"Right why these?"

"Well we've done a full assault on these, we've 'ad a small tickle on 'em, it was easy pickings, their security is full of holes, it'll be a cinch, now we've gotta 'ave split-second timing. We gotta coordinate the raid to work together, confusion with the 'ole bill is the only way it'll work, with all this going on they ain't got the manpower or back up to chase four incidents at once, by the time they cotton on to centralise their retaliation we're home and away"

There is a pause the group round the table look at one another not quite believing what they have heard, one of the gang starts to speak, Albert motions him to be silent. He starts to tap his cigar on the table, it is the only noise in the room, he looks Alice in the eyes, she stares him out, he slowly smiles, then slings himself back in his chair, laughing out loud.

"I like it, in fact I love it, Alice you are a diamond, champagne for all"

"George, I can rely on my girls to get the merchandise but the only thing that bothers me is when my girls run out onto the street I don't want them standing there looking like a bleeding pack of ponies waiting for a bus, your getaway boys gotta be there straining at the leash"

"Alice don't worry my boys won't let you down, will you boys?"

They all nod their heads.

"Now drink up, we got a lot to celebrate"

Friday morning: Albert gets a message that two of his drivers have been arrested down "The Cut" for playing "Chase the Lady"

With a group of tourists

He phones Alice, suggesting they raid only two stores

"No it won't work, the idea is to overload their response , if we only blag two stores they'll be onto us, haven't you go any back up?"

"I'll look into it, get back to you later"

A phone call to Sam from Albert breaks up his concentration on a crossword puzzle.

"Sam y'know I mentioned we might need a driver? Well now I do, come round to "East Street Market" in an hour, you can familiarise yourself with the motor."

Sam duly arrives at the market, a group of young people are admiring a large Austin Saloon, Sam eases his way through the throng, to the driver

"Jump in, we're going for a spin, you driving"

Sam takes to the wheel, being ordered up to the "Elephant & Castle", he is told to go round the roundabout once, then again, the passenger letting him go faster on each visit. Satisfied, he is then ordered to go down a stretch of road to turn corners at a fast speed. This exercise went on for two hours, he is told to pull over, the passenger nods his head.

"You'll do, meet us tonight at Albert's pub seven o'clock sharp"

ALBERTS PUB: THAT NIGHT

The gang are seated round the table, Albert at the head, Sam sits on an empty chair, he is not the last one to come in, that was left to the man who had taken him on the driving assessment, looks at Sam, goes over to Albert bends down to speak in his ear, Albert just nods his head, he goes to walk back to a vacant chair.

"Right boys, this is going to be our first enterprise with Alice an' the "Forty Thieves""

The group sniggers

"It ain't no laughing matter, pay attention! Tomorrow we gonna hit four different targets. You'll all be told the location 'alf 'n' hour before we hit 'em, make sure your motors are tanked up, fully reliable, I don't want any of my clients left stranded on the pavement, I've gotta reputation to think of, you've got your balls to think of, you know what I mean, right, the next time we meet is when you get a 0phone call for the rendezvous, that's it; Sam, I wanna word with yuh."

Sam walks over, the remnants shuffle over to the bar

"Danny tells me you done alright on your little training course, it'' be the real thing tomorrow, you feel up to it?"

Sam nods.

"That's what I like to hear, positives, now let's drink to our success."

Sam is now in a dilemma, he has to get word to Foden that something big is going down, making his excuses about getting an early night, he leaves. Dan looks over to Albert, who nods, waiting for Sam to go out of the door he pursues him, keeping in the shadows, Sam hails a cab, "Waterloo Station"

Danny jumps in his car to follow him at a safe distance, stopping at a cab rank, Sam gets out into the flow of traffic, runs up the public stairway, a baggage trolley trundles past, Sam jumps on one of the barrows pushing himself into the mailbags, Danny runs on to the platform looking round the trolley, goes within six feet of him, coming to the end of the platform, Sam jumps off walks quickly through an interconnecting passage way, out on to the main road to hail a taxi.

Outside the police station he uses the public emergency phone. Several minutes later Foden appears, keeping in the shadows Sam gets up close to him, telling him about the earlier conversation he had.

"Haven't you got an inkling or anything I can work on?"

"Nothing, if I can get to a phone before the off, I'll try"

"Yuh, be careful, I don't want to jeopardise everything for a silly mistake or decision, now we've got a small foothold in the organisation."

They both walk away in opposite directions.

11 O'CLOCK SATURDAY MORNING

Sam is waiting on the corner of East Street. A car pulls up, driven by the same man who took him on his assessment course. He moves over to let Sam take the wheel.

"Right drive on"

"Where to?"

"I'll tell you as we go"

After twenty five minutes of driving, they are driving slowly down Bayswater Road, "Whiteleys" the large store is at the end of the road.

"Turn left next"

Sam obeys following the road

"Okay turn around, pull over to the kerb, cut the engine"

The accomplice gets out a newspaper starts to read. After several minutes Sam enquires what they're doing there

"Just be ready to start the engine when I tell you, that's all you got to know. Looking in his mirror the co-driver see's the image of a policeman walking slowly towards them,

"Bollocks"

Sam looks into his mirror, from around the corner, a mounted policeman stops to talk to the uniformed policeman who slowly walks towards the car, the co-driver slowly folds his paper, from a dashboard compartment he retrieves a pistol, slowly hides it under the newspaper. A tapping on the window draws his attention, the policeman gesticulates to lower the window.

"Can you tell me what your business is sir? As you could be blocking up the road in an emergency"

"Yes officer if I could explain, my wife and her friends are just picking up their wedding dresses and as the boxes are quite large to get into a cab, as soon as they come out of the store, any minute now, I'll pull down to pick them up"

The policeman pauses, looks up and down the street,

"Okay but don't be here too long"

"Yes officer, thank you"

He turns to walk back to the mounted policeman, making sure he's out of sight the gangster slowly puts the gun back.

"I know what you're thinking, would I have used it if he got too busy, cause I would"

Sam looks straight ahead, the gangster throws the paper on the floor in front of them, three women are running towards them.

"Start the engines, go towards the girls!!"

Sam starts the car, slams it into gear, careers down the road, stopping exactly adjacent to the trio, the gangster jumps out opens the doors, the girls unceremoniously pile in on top of one another laughing, and he slams the door.

"Right let's get out of here!"

As they pass the store door, three store detectives run out looking up and down the road, seeing the policeman they shout, wave, he blows his whistle, runs towards them, the mounted policeman takes up the chase, following in hot pursuit, the gangster laughs,

"Er look at this, its Tom Mix chasing after the baddies"

The girls look through the window, chortling,

"well this is one time he won't get the bad guys"

"You mean he won't get the bad girls"

They laugh.

Sam taking orders reverses, up to Hyde Park Corner, forces his way into a stream of traffic who give way, carrying on down to Park lane then Piccadilly, going South towards Westminster Bridge to South London.

"Okay slow down we've lost 'em"

Sam takes a look in his mirror, the girls had sorted themselves out, sitting comfortably, he takes a second glance, it was Rose, she leans forward so that her face is reflected in the whole mirror. Sam is taken aback, he goes to turn his head, the gangster taps his shoulder.

"Keep your mince's looking to the front"

"Nice driving Sam, you could be my private getaway chauffer anytime"

She falls back, the girls laugh.

The central London police headquarters were getting inundated with the same emergency message from three other stores at the same time:- four of London's top West End stores had been targeted by the same "Bourne and Hollingsworth", "Derry and Toms", "Whiteleys", and "Army and Navy" stores.

It was a hopeless scenario, the police just didn't have the manpower, the pursuing police cars, didn't have the speed to catch their quarries. It was a complete fiasco. Foden was looking out of his window when one of his detectives brought in the last message, without turning he orders him to read it.

"The last raid was at "Whiteleys", sir, a policeman tried to abscond the getaway vehicle, closely followed by a mounted policeman, but they got clean away....."

"What'd you bleeding expect? If it was the four horsemen of the apocalypse they still wouldn't have caught them"

"It seems like it was planned like a military operation sir"

"Do you know detective, you're in the wrong job, you should be in military intelligence"

"Yes sir"

He walks out.

The first of the getaway cars pulled up outside Alice's house, the girls jumped out, pulling tight as they could, their overburdened coats, the last girl in the car pulls away, Sam was the second car at the rendezvous, the driver telling him he would take over the driving, Sam gets out helping Rose, she hugs him.

"Quick Sam come inside we'll have a drink to celebrate"

All the contraband is laid out on the large table in the front room, Alice slowly looking over all the items. A knock on the door, the third group tumble in.

"Alice, the last car had to make a detour on account of a hold-up at Kings Cross, unloading the cattle going up York Way, the driver took the girls over to Albert's Place, we'll bring 'em over when the fuss dies down a bit"

"Well girls you've done yourselves proud this time, four stores, Christmas has come early, there'll be a little bonus for you all with this lot, right now let's have a drink, Sam can I have a word?"

Sam saunters over

"On the face of it your performance was good, everybody home safe 'n' sound in one piece..... if your interested can I say, welcome to the club?"

"I would be honoured Alice, when can I start?"

They laugh, Rose catches his eye he walks her to her, kisses her on the cheek.

NEXT MORNING

Foden is about to knock on the door of the Commissioner's office, a detective walks past, "out of the corner of his mouth"

"To hell with your luck, he's in a right two 'n' eight"

Foden is standing in front of his peer.

"What the blazes is going on? I was pulled before the Home Secretary last night at the ladies night, he wants to know who these people are, it's like a bloody rehearsal episode from a wild west film, he told me in no uncertain terms he wants some quick results:- I want them damn well quicker, we've got some local elections coming up directly, how do you think the electorate is going to vote, if they can't go shopping without the fear of being herder, yes I sad herder around in the course of their leisure time?"

"Sir, I've got a detective on the case as we speak sir, he's infiltrated the circle but everything is decided on a whom to know basis....."

"I don't care about whose to know, I want results, quick, so does the minister, you understand?"

"Yes sir"

A DAY LATER, MORNING

At the prearranged meeting Sam and Foden have met at Smithfield Market, keeping a safe distance initially, they both have bags of meat, Foden goes into a pub, orders a drink then goes to sit in a secluded corner, several minutes later, Sam casually walks in orders his drink, slowly walks through the crowded bar of meat-porters to sit down, with a distance between them, next to Foden, gets a newspaper out prepares to read it.

"I'm getting an arse full of dialogue from up top, they want results or he's threatened to pull the plug on the operation, you've got anything to substantiate my position?"

Sam slowly folds his paper.

"I couldn't forewarn you of the latest escapade but it was incognitos right to the last minute, they didn't let me out of their sights"

"Right, obviously they run a tight ship, keep at it, 'soon as you get a sniff at their next caper, sign in straight away."

He finishes his drink, walks off leaving his bag of meat from across the other side of the bar, once of Albert's gang slowly gazes around the pub, he focuses on Sam, not going over, he watches Sam's movements until he finishes his drink, exits, leaving the two bags on the seat.

NEXT MORNING – CHELSEA

Rose and Sam are walking down the Kings Road, they enter a high lass ladies fashion house, the staff comes to greet her.

"Miss Rose, so glad to see you again, you're looking divine:- how may we help?"

"I would like to see your latest evening wear if I may?"

"Certainly, I'll get the model to show you the latest collection"

On the way out Sam is in a jaunting mood.

"Tell me Rose, don't take this personally....."

"I always take you personally Sam, you know that"

"Well with all the contraband that you borrow from the shop, surely there must be enough there must be enough there to choose from"

She laughs

"Sam, it's an unwritten statement that us girls never wear any of it, what's that word you used? Contraband, that we have, we like to buy our own clothes, it's just part of the thing we do"

Sam looks at her quizzically,

"To make it more easy for you to understand, I'll take you to the flicks tomorrow, there's a film I'd like you to see. Let's go up West, finish of the day in a nice restaurant:- my treat"

They hail a taxi

THAT NIGHT: ALBERTS PUB

Albert is listening intently to the man who had spotted Sam in the pub; Albert is tapping his finger on the table slowly nodding his head.

Sam is walking from his lodgings, a large car pulls up beside him, the door opens

"Jump in"

He pauses; jumps in, his mind racing, thinking where he must have made a mistake or error of judgement. They arrive in silence at Albert's pub, are led by one man, Sam in the middle, flanked by two men, enter the office

"Nice to see you Sam, sit down"

He sits opposite Albert, from behind the two bags of meat are unceremoniously dropped on the table.

"Now if my nose 'n' eyes serve me right the contents of these bags contain perfectly good meat..... whatd'ya think?" Sam has to think quick, gets out a cigarette, a hand from behind lights it.

"The meats alright, but it was the wrong type, if you look closely you'll find that they were cuts of lamb, my dogs only eat beef, you should know Albert, what do your pals feed their dogs on?"

"Don't be clever Sam, why did you leave the bags after you paid good money for them, you could have taken them home.... and who was the other punter next to you"

"We both brought the parcels from a bummeroon, no questions asked, you know that, he just happened to be behind me, probably looked like a good deal to hi as well, some you win, some you lose...."

"It looked like that you lost that one, why'd ya leave the parcel behind then?"

"Did your man tell you there were a couple of market police by the door as we walked in, if we had got collared by 'em we would have got barred from the market, no receipt, the bummeroon would have been nicked, lose his job, anyway you know the price in the butchers, I wouldn't be able to but it retail, have to give up my dogs"

Albert looks round to his entourage, nods a small sack is thrown on the table in front of Sam, he looks credulously at it

"What's that?"

"That Sam, my boy, is what your departed head would be wrapped up in, to be found floating by the Isle of Dogs tomorrow morning if your explanation didn't add up, you savvy?"

"Yes Sam, okay we got that little incident out of the way, let's get down to business"

"Listen Albert I don't like this kind of interrogation or accusation, if you don't trust me, I might as well be on my way now"

"Don't take it to heart Sam, we run a very tight ship here, we have to be careful who we employ in the firm, so having cleared the air, I got a proposition to make to you, how would you like to be a regular driver for me? Judging you on your ability the other day, maybe with a little tweaking to polish up your knowledge of London you could be an asset to me?"

"Yuh that seems alright by me, and if I get seen in different situations, what don't add up, just ask me"

"Don't push it Sam, by the way, that Rose is a nice girl, look after her"

NEXT DAY: IN THE CINEMA

Sam has his arm around Rose, the film is "Flying Down to Rio"

"Now Sam you see what I mean about these flappers enjoying themselves, the parties, restaurants they go to, living on the edge, that's why I like to buy my own clothes, dresses, what we nick from the stores it seems like second hand, but you not being a women you wouldn't understand that, would you?"

"I guess not Rose, but I'll take you as you are, and it's a bit early for a party, I'll escort you to a nice restaurant later in the governors car, it won't be living on the edge, but it's a good second choice"

She laughs, squeezes his hand.

TWO DAYS LATER – RESTAURANT IN THE WEST END

Alice and Albert are seated around a table, two members of his gang are positioned adjacently so that their privacy is guarded.

"Albert everything is going well, you agree? Well I've heard from one of our shouts that a lot of pressure from up top is being put on the force, taking a very special interest in our occupations, so what I suggest is that we tone down our operations until the vested interests of the old bill calm down – agreed?"

"Agreed, but what can we do in the interim?"

"I've got a lot of punters crying out for the merchandise"

"I'm coming to that, what I propose is that we target smaller towns, outside the city of London's old bill"

"Yuh that's alright but what you gonna do when you've got all the tot, 'ow d'you propose you get back to the Elephant? They'd just radio ahead, and then nick yuh"

"Okay what I wanna do is get a collection of empty suitcases, drop em off at the left luggage offices at the local train station, then our hoisters would load up the merchandise after going shopping."

"What'd you think – good?"

"Do you know what Alice, sometimes I'm lost for words how your brain ticks over, I wouldn't like to be your enemy, what do I think? It's bleeding marvellous, when d'we start?"

"Well I've got to sort out the finer details, take a couple of dummy runs; the main thing is we got to use your best drivers"

"That's not a problem, why don't you take Sam on your first tryout, he's come on alright?"

"Okay he can bring Rose along, she'd make a good decoy, they're getting on alright"

"That maybe Alice, but don't let passion get in the way of business"

They both laugh

A NIGHT CLUB:

A small number of the gang are at a table. A group of men, half inebriated walk over to the table to introduce themselves, explaining that they have had a very beneficial day on the stock exchange. They bring a table over so that they are immersed in each other's company, after a while they pair off into two private booths, left to their own devices. One of the girls Dolly, leaves with one of the male group. They later end up at a hotel. After a short while they are in bed together, suddenly the door opens, Dolly jumps up pulls the bed clothes off the bed, the man in shock completely naked, a flash from the camera brings him back to reality, Dolly is quickly getting her clothes on

"You bitch!"

"Your right there, but you'll be hearing from this bitch in the near future, good night ducky"

The two heavies guard her exit, as she leaves.

A TRAIN STATION IN THE SUBURBS: DAY

Three women pull up, call a porter to take three large suitcases to the left luggage offices, he gladly complies, they give him a large tip.

An hour later another car pulls up, he takes the ticket to the left luggage to retrieve the three suitcases. Sam refuses the offer of the station porter to put the cases in the car, tipping him to lure him away, accordingly when the porter goes back to his office, Rose jumps out putting the suitcases in the back of the car, it was full up with merchandise where she had been "shopping earlier"

"Quick Sam let's get out of here"

Sam swerves the high powered car out of the car park onto the main road, bells ringing announce the pursuing constabulary, a few minutes away, Sam accelerates the car, turning into a country lane, the police car in his mirror starts to get larger, he comes to a roundabout, at the last minute he swerves to his left, the pursuing police car loses control, careers across the roundabout plummeting into a hedge, Rose roars with laughter, Sam smiles.

"You can be my private chauffer ay time big boy"

She kisses him on the back of the neck.

TWO DAYS LATER: LONDON STOCK EXCHANGE

A man and a woman walk into the foyer, they approach the enquiry desk. "Can I help you sir?"

"Yes I'd like to speak to Mr Chappstick"

The concierge goes to a directory, then rings,

"Whom should I say calling sir"

"An associated whom he met at a party two nights ago"

"He'll be down in a few minutes; would you please follow me into a guest lounge?"

They position themselves on a table, Chappstick enters, on seeing the couple his confident aura vanishes, recognising the women who he had liaisons with earlier looking nervously around, he struts forward.

"Now look here, who the hell do you think you're dealing with, do you know who I am?"

"I know who the hell we're dealing with, you're the deputy manager of Schol and company, the largest underwriters at Lloyds, also we know where you live, your wife and children, very comfortable"

The man gestures him to sit down, puts a leather briefcase on the table, from which he extrudes a brown envelope, slowly putting a photo on the table, he looks at it, slumps full back in his chair in silence, shaking his head, putting his fingers to his mouth the man reaches for another photo to lay on the table in front of him, a waiter walks over asking if they need a drink, Chappstick lunges forward to hide the images,

"No no" the waiter walks off perplexed at the treatment

"Mr Chappstick I have several more exposures, if you would like these to be posted to your company's board and to your wife, it's up to you"

"What do you want?"

"I want one thousand pounds in two days time in a package, I'll phone you in the morning for the drop off; if by any chance you decide to go to the authorities I'll not hesitate to dispatch the photos I have mentioned, do you understand?"

He nods, the man and women get up to leave. "Hope it doesn't cloud your judgment and decision today: it's a good insurance policy"

Two hours later the man enters Albert's pub "How'd it go?"

"Sweet as a nut"

Chapter 5

SAME DAY, ALICE'S HOUSE

Sam is holding court with Alice, the girls are trying on the dresses, accessories from their latest venture.

"Well Sam, Rose tells me your last little escapade was something like "The Keystone Cops", at the same speed as well"

"Yes Albert it was a bit hectic, nothing like going down Oxford Street"

"Well it proves my theory, we'll do some more of those operations, going to different areas, the ol' bill won't ever know where we're gonna hit 'em next"

"Seems good to me Alice"

"When we've got 'em into a false sense of security, we'll start taking on up West again"

"When d'you think that'll be Alice?"

She looks at him, pauses, taps him on the nose

"That's for me to know, and for you to wait and see"

A DAY LATER: EMBANKMENT NIGHT. COFFEE STALL

Sam, Foden are a few feet apart, looking forward

"The thing is guv I think I'm being slowly trusted, I don't wanna mess things up by being too pushy, Alice, Albert, keep their cards close to their chests, I've just got to find a way to prompt their next move"

"What about this Rose girl?"

"What about her?"

"Well by what you've told me, she's pretty close to Alice, anyway she could come across? Like telling you what their next objective is?"

"Yuh I'll work on it, but nurturing her and not going over the top is a fine line"

"Work at it, keep in touch"

Foden leaves, Sam leaves five minutes later in the opposite direction.

INTERIOR OF LARGE HOUSE IN CHELSEA.

One of Alice's girls is being interviewed by the lady of the house, they are seated opposite one another.

Finally, in silence, the owner looks up smiles to tell the job-seeker that her references are quite in order; she explains the hours, rate of pay, suggesting she starts at the beginning of the next week. The girl makes her exit. At the end of the road she turns to make sure she is not being followed, parked on the other side of one of Albert's cars, gets in]

"How'd it go?"

"Got it, start next week"

"Good girl, give me the references, we can use them again"

The car pulls away

TWO DAYS LATER: KNIGHTSBRIDGE

Two women walk out of a large store, walking quickly before the store detectives can pinpoint them, walking briskly, keeping close to the shop windows, they fail to notice four of Alice's girls walking behind them, at the next shop doorway they surround them, hustling them into a corner

"Right you two this is our patch, hand over the schmutter!!"

"Piss off!"

"Y'what? Piss off!"

One of the girls punches the women in the face, the other girl starts to retaliate but is bludgeoned to the ground, the shoplifting garment falls open to reveal the stolen goods, the assailants quickly gather them up, depositing them in their own garments, leaving the two women in a huddle,

"If I catch you again on our patch you'll end up in Charing Cross Hospital"

Two of the girls gets hold of their coats, trying them, ripping them in half: the girls go off in different directions to be lost in the pedestrian throng.

THE HOUSE IN CHELSEA

It's half way through the week that the house maid had started, the lady of the house summons her to her main room.

"My dear I have to go to the theatre, I'll be several hours, but I would like the beds turned down but have the hot water bottles ready"

"Yes Madam"

Looking through the side of the curtained window, the maid watches the chauffeured car pull away. She runs up to her bedroom, from under her bed she extracts a large carpet bag, goes to the master bedroom where she systematically puts all the silver hair brushes, jewellery, and perfume bottles, goes through the dressing room table drawers, putting in anything of value, then to the bedroom side table, putting in an ornate clock, going to the wardrobe, she flicks through the garments picks out a fox fur, tries it around her neck, leaves it on, glancing around the room, there is nothing else of interest or is too large to take, quickly going down stairs, she goes to the kitchen, from a cupboard she extracts a wedding gift cutlery set, then a set of silver salt and pepper pots, quickly she goes into the main room, a carriage clock gets her attention, the bag is now full, smiling she walks over to a small bureau, moving her hands over the small drawers, copying which she witnessed the owner operating, a low click, a hidden compartment opens, to reveal a jewellery box, this is quickly disposed in the bag, she goes to the window again, arranged by a pre-arranged telephone call, a car pulls up outside, she walks briskly to the front door, opens it, walks out, waves, blows a kiss, smiles, jumps in the car.

"Home James, or maybe to the theatre" Sarcastically

NEXT DAY SPEAK EASY

Sam, Rose are seated at a table, the atmosphere is high key, men, women are dancing the latest craze, they are holding each other's hand across the table.

"Well Rose I'm beginning to like you a little bit, not too much, just a little bit"

"Well sailor I'm beginning to like you a little, but much"

They both laugh.

"Rose how long d'you want to carry on the life style you're acting out now? I realise it's exciting, the clothes, jewellery, the friendship your experiences with the girls, I really understand, but it does worry me, that when you and the girls' luck runs out, maybe you get caught: they would take all your previous escapades into consideration, you're looking at a long stretch."

She looks at him, takes a long drag on her long cigarette holder, picks up her cocktail glass empties it, then splays her fingers on the table, displaying all the jewellery on her fingers, then points to her shoes pulling her dress above her ankles, turns to face Sam kissing him fully on the lips, running her fingers through his hair.

"That says it all really"

She turns to watch the dance floor, a slow number stats, sung by a coloured singer, she gets up, without asking, a man on another table to dance, Sam is taken back, trying to get his head around the situation, Rose dancing with a perfect stranger, doesn't take her eyes off Sam, he is transfixed. The dance over, she saunters back to the table, his date is not happy.

"Sam you've got to understand, I'm a free spirit, these last couple of years have been the happiest of my life, before what I'm doing, what I'm involved with, girls around here would cut their right arm off for:- when I was kid, me, my sisters, we had nothing, living on hand me downs from the mission people, foraging around the markets every night to bring home food, my mum died of TB, dad got killed in a gang fight:- Rose came along showed me a way out, there's no way I'm going back, anyway I'm not squandering all the money I've made, its put away, when I've got enough I'm going to open a high couture women's dress shop in Knightsbridge"

"Does Alice know, what I mean is after all the training, the angles, it must take time to bring the girls up to standard, not withstanding you might get caught before your ready to retire"

"I don't wanna go there, be positive, let's dance, tomorrow's another day"

ONE DAY LATER: INSIDE COURT ROOM

One of the girls of the gang has been arrested; she is called to the dock. Alice is with Rose in the public gallery, Alice whispers in Rose's ear.

"This should make you smile"

"Can you tell the court if there are nay mitigating circumstances?"

"Well I mitigate that I'm not guilty"

The court laughs, the magistrate calls to order.

"Could you tell the court in your own words how the numbered items on the bench came to be in your possession, and why you had no receipts when you were apprehended by the store detective?"

"Well your honour the items you mentioned were to be for presents and I wanted to impress my friends so that they would not know the price"

She then burst into tears, clearly the magistrate could see through this charade, and displayed a sympathetic stance.

"Does the prosecution have any more evidence or accusations they wish to put forward before I pronounce sentencing?"

The solicitor stands up

"Yes we do, we wish to call the store detective who apprehended the accused"

Betty quickly stops her crying as she exchanges position with the store detective in the witness box

"Will you please tell the court what you found in the large carpet bag what the accused was carrying?"

"When we apprehended the accused with the Fox stole we found in her bag, twenty stolen items which she had no receipt for, consequently we called for the police and she was arrested."

The judges face took a sterner turn, not for the stolen items, but nearly been taken in by her professional act, he stared at her, ordering her back into the witness box,

"You'll serve four months, take her down"

This time the crocodile tears were for real.

WALKING TOWARDS THE SERPENTINE

Sam had just passed the band stand carrying a newspaper, he was about for a meet with Foden, waiting for the band to finish their number, he casually walks to the back, his sixth sense tells him he is being followed, he didn't want to be observed meeting Foden, he had to think quick, walking slowly to a sandy stretch road where the Kings Troop train their horses, he was in luck, a large troop was coming towards him, he gages the distance between the gates on the other side, he had to get across, owing that the vast expanse of Hyde Park did not offer him any cover, as Foden could appear at any moment at their agreed rendezvous; waiting for the trotting horses to get within his anticipated judgement, he made a dash in front of the leading horse, two of them rear up, the commander shouts abuse at him, once safely across he runs to the gates, hiding behind one of the pillars, peering back, he sees his adversary looking forlornly for any sign of him, slowly walks away in the direction he came. Sam continues his walk along the road until he reaches the Albert memorial, Foden is on the other side of the square sitting down reading a newspaper, noticing Sam walking towards him, he casually folds up the newspaper depositing it in a waste paper bin, this was the signal that their liaison could go ahead, Sam sits next to him.

"Well, got anything for me?"

"Nothing solid at the moment, I've got push to my situation with Rose, Alice tells her everything, if I can get her complete trust concerning the gangs next move, we could bag the lot all in one go."

"Work at it, you phone me when you're completely sure, the commissioners strangling my balls, he wants results or he'll pull the whole operation off"

They both leave in opposite directions.

DAYS LATER. CHELTENHAM RACE COURSE

Rose, Sam now look like the respectable couple they are walking arm in arm through the saddling enclosure, Albert had furnished them with members badges, Sam quietly indulging in the admiring glances Rose is attracting.

"Do you know any of these punters, or are you just trying to make me jealous?"

Rose smiles

"No, it's just that I usually come with Alice and Albert, they're just paying their respects"

"That's alright then"

"Sam I'm just going to have a small flutter on horse Albert gave me a tip for, shall I put something on for you?"

"If you like"

Sam focuses his binoculars on the rails, a hand goes across his field of vision, he lowers the binoculars,

"Hello sergeant, or is it inspector yet?"

Sam has to think quickly, it's one of his snitches from London; he turns to see Rose in conversation with the bookie.

"Listen, listen good, I'm involved with a lady, who I shouldn't be involved with, I shouldn't even be here, now 'eres five quid, go 'n' enjoy yourself you haven't seen me right? Or else I'll be calling in a few favours, now you scarper"

"Certainly Mr Ford, I haven't seen a thing" He walks off, looking back once.

"Who's that unsavoury character Sam? It wouldn't do to be seen with the likes of the working class, after all, we are highly flighty aren't we?"

They both laugh, making their way to the members bar.

IN THE BEDROOM – ROSE'S HOUSE

Rose, Sam are in bed, Rose is smoking,

"Rose when's the next escapade, I'm beginning to miss the excitement?"

"That's strange, when I first met you, you were very laid back, didn't want to get involved, now you're like a staffy tearing at the leash – I think Alice an' Albert are on the edge of planning a big one then going to lay off for a while, she wants all the girls to meet at Albert's club tomorrow night, you'll probably be involved but I can't say anymore, cause I don't know myself, whenever it is it could be a bit more dangerous than what we're used to"

"Haven't you got any idea at all?"

Rose looks at him quizzingly

"What are you, some kind of copper, and all these questions?"

MUNITIONS FACTORY, THAT NIGHT

Two of Albert's gang are in the act of breaking into the armoury, carefully going through the labelled boxes, they check their list until they come across what they are searching for, smoke canisters, star shells, carefully putting a dozen or so of each item in a canvas rucksack, they backtrack the way they had entered the building, waiting to get into a waiting car, to leave.

THE NEXT NIGHT INSIDE THE CLUB

Albert, Rose and two of his close confidents are looking over a large exploded diagram, on close inspection it is the layout of a large store interior construction, Albert folds the map up to centre on one section, it is the money office, tapping his finger,

"It'll be a walkover - surprises, professionalism, speed, all in our favour, what you reckon Alice?"

"Well it's never been attempted before so that's in our favour at least"

"Call the people to order Bernard"

Bernard calls the ensemble to order, the girls stop laughing, giggling and the men put down their drinks.

"Right everybody pay attention..."

From behind him Albert uncovers a blackboard to reveal a plan of the cash office.

"This is what we're going to hit tomorrow, it's their last day of the month cashing up, paying out wages and money from the sales"

He picks up one of the canisters. "This is a smoke bomb, harmless out in a field but in a closed environment will cause a little bit of a panic, confusion to the unexpected, what we intend to do is put a couple in the vacuum canisters that take the money into the cash office, also dropping a couple in the store to keep the store detectives occupied, also we got a few star shells, just to brighten things up a little bit." The group laugh

"Alice is going to go through it with her girls, they'll take their special dresses, large carpet bags, the boys' look after the money, the girls should get a good haul of schmutter, just to add to the confusion we'll put the sprinklers on, the getaway will be handled by our drivers, we'll all split to different address's keep the coppers on their tails, any questions?"

"When's it gonna happen?" asks a voice from the back

"Tomorrow, I want all the drivers at ten o'clock at the club just to finalise details, Alice will place her girls in position so that everything co-ordinates, that's all you got to know till tomorrow, more important make sure the cars are in tip-top condition so that they start on the touch of the button, we don't want a cochel of girls in the back with their bloomers full of cabbage with the old bill feeling their collars, it wouldn't be lady like"

LATER THAT NIGHT IN THE RESTAURANT

"Well Rose it looks like this could be the big one"

"Could be right Sam, but between you and me Alice reckons if we can pull this caper off successfully, make a little nest egg for ourselves we'll lie low for a while. We can't keep carrying on like this, our luck's got to run out sometime"

"What would you do?"

"Well I've been thinking about it for a while, I'd move away from the Elephant, get a nice little high class salon in Pimlico, importing the latest fashions from the continent, that were I reckon it's going to happen, with all these latest dance crazes, the film stars wearing all the latest styles, the bright young things wanting to keep up with them and all, me just keeping a low profile, no worries."

"Y'know what Rose, you've got a very clever head on those shoulders, d'you need a chaperone, or a handyman-driver, maybe?"

Rose laughs

"I've got one already; let's dance to our success, hopefully."

EARLY MORNING NEXT DAY

Sam is at a coffee stall at a cab rank; Foden appears a few minutes later, they stand at the rank, looking in different directions, Foden reading a newspaper.

"This is going to be the big one guv, can't give you all the info on it, we're meeting at ten o'clock this morning at the club, the only thing I can suggest is that you'll have to disperse your team as best you can until you know what start their gonna take"

"Can't do it – ain't got the man power, I'll have to shadow you when you come out of the club"

"It's risky"

"I know, what can I do, it's the only chance I got of nabbing the Elephant boys 'n' the Forty Thieves in one go, can't afford not to take up the opportunity, the commissioner going to disperse the operation at the end of the week, I'll do my best to keep out of harm, don't greet me with open arms if you recognise me"

CLUB LATER THAT MORNING

Sam enters the bar looks around, some of the faces were familiar, others he didn't recognise. Albert walks onto the platform at the front of entourage. He stands next to a table which has a cloth covering some items.

"Right listen up, some of the faces here you won't know, that's good, they're some associates from North London, they're gonna do the blag, the other fellows are gonna plant the smoke bombs in the cash canisters, maybe let off a star shell here 'n' there, that leaves my men to be ready in the cars, when they run out you can take 'em to the rendezvous that I'll explain in a minute, now listen carefully, this operation will only be successful if we all keep to a strict timetable – Jack here will hand you an envelope each, the driver will do what he does best, his passenger will open the letter at eleven thirty precisely, don't veer from any of the directions: enough said, now we'll all stay here till eleven fifteen, have a little drink"

Sam looks around then sees who his partner is, its Lewis the one person he does not get on with

"It looks like we gotta be bosom pals, until this is over"

"You reckon"

Sam walks away to get a drink, Lewis follows behind him but does not drink at the bar with him.

SAME TIME: ALICE'S HOUSE

All the girls are putting the finishing adjustments to their garments, making sure the large pockets are easily accessible; Rose is in conversation with Alice.

"Alice I reckon I'm gonna lay low after today's jaunt, we've been lucky up to yet, be nice if we could go out on a high"

"Have you got something you've gotta tell me young lady? You seem to be on high lately, is that Sam getting through to you?"

"It's not that Alice, well maybe, I don't wanna sound old fashioned, but he's kind, considerate, treats me well"

"Good for you, let's see what happens after today, we'll have a cosy chat later"

They both embrace.

ELEVEN O'CLOCK. THAT MORNING

At two minute intervals five cars pull up behind Selfridges, parking on different sides of the road, the girls walk into the side of the road, the girls walk into the side entrances, while two other groups gain entrance by way of the front entrance, the store detectives don't give them a second glance, coming up from the Regent Street end, a charabanc stops, across the other side of the road, the men disgorge themselves from the charabanc, they divide themselves into small groups some go individually to enter the store. Once inside they go in different directions, splitting up individually.

Alice, Rose, her group slowly start looking over the articles in the perfume department, Alice looks at her watch, the group look at one another in unison, and recognition, the other groups of girls are all positioned at strategic points around the store, their leader also checking their watches. The male gang members slowly regroup, avoiding any quick suspicious moves, they are in the tailoring department, buying small articles insisting they have large bags for their purchases, others of the group have top coats over their arms, the large clock outside rings half past eleven, as if from nowhere two of the gang jump up onto a large display unit, whilst they wait until two of the vacuum cylinders come hurling towards them, they throw a coat over the wires stopping them, from inside the stores base, they produce two cylinders, pull the percussion caps off, directing the slowly smoking canister in the direction of the cash office, jumping down, mingle individually with the punters, Alice, Rose her group have now mover onto the fur coats department, going to each sales assistant so that there is no one available, making their presence felt, all trying on different coats, the assistants, security minded, keep a close countenance to them, this leaves other members of the gang ready to hike the unguarded coats when the star shells go off.

Inside the cash office, the air is thick with smoke, the gang have put on the gas masks, retrieved from their bags of purchase, and the money is all stacked up in neat piles, quickly scooped into bags, the cash tellers are blinded by the smoke, clearing the office of its contents, the gang walk out closing the door behind them. Discarding their masks they make their getaway by way of the auxiliary lift, to the next floor, finding the passage they want, they come to an open window, looking down are four of the gang, dropping the proceeds weighed down by the smoke masks, they quickly fall into the arms of the gang, grabbing the loot, they race to one of the cars and speed off.

In the store it is in turmoil, two star shells are let off creating more havoc, and confusion. Alice, Rose for their part quickly grab the coats they are trying on pushing them into their large coats at the same time the others girls, barge into the bewildered assistants, allowing Alice, with her group to walk quickly to the side entrances, the heat off the star shells had now set off the sprinklers, adding more mayhem to an already bizarre situation. This suited the gang down to the ground, the store detective's decisions were in turmoil, panic had set in, where did they start, the head detective tried the phones, the line was dead, the other girl gang members on the other floors also had a field day, making good their escape in the same organised fashion, breaking out into the street they slowly walked up the street to get in the waiting cars slowly pulling away in different directions.

"Can't we close the doors? That's the only way to stop them"

"No it's against the law, there's no fire"

The chief store detective sat down held his head in his hands, his subordinates formed a small group around him, frustrated they slowly walked away.

The men who raided the cash office made good their escape by way of going on to the roof, then down the fire escape stairs to ground where they filtered into the throng on the public, some getting on the omnibuses, or hailing a cab, to disappear into thin air.

Alice, Rose, her group got into Sam's car, he heads towards Marble Arch then down Park Lane towards Knightsbridge.

"Sam could we possibly stop at Harrods? I fancy a nice meal, plus the fact it'll strengthen our alibi"

Sam drives around the back of Harrods, he keeps close company with Alice, Rose after pulling the fur coats from their coats, pulling the back seat forward, they dispose of the loot.

"Right ladies, I want you to be on your best behaviour, no smoke bombs or star shells"

"Wouldn't dream of it". They nearly chirp in unison

THAT NIGHT TEN O'CLOCK, ALICES HOUSE

A party in full swing, Sam is in close liaison with Rose, slowly the noise filters down they all look towards the doorway, the house occupant's move slowly back as Foden makes his entrance, flanked by several policemen.

"Hello Alice, hope you're enjoying yourselves, mind if I have a look around?"

"Only if you have a warrant"

He nods turns his head, one of the policemen hands Alice a piece of paper

"Happy? Right lads, start at the top, give it a good turn over, I don't want anybody to leave, one of my constables will be taking statements to clarify your alibis, it'll be a waste of time, but its protocol."

He slowly looks around the room, Sam puts a glass to his face, not from Foden, but one of the constables might have seen at the police station, he turns his head towards Rose, she nestles up to him.

"Protect me Sam"

She giggles

Foden hears it, turns to Sam for a quick glimpse. After five minutes the constables come down.

"All clear sir, nothing up there"

"Okay, well Alice I'll be checking all the alibis, one day you'll slip up"

"I hope you'll be there detective"

The house occupants laugh, the police leave

"Well what was that all about?"

Asks one of the girls

"Don't you worry, it's just that they have to justify to their superiors that they're up to the mark, keeping tabs on South London's most successful organised collection of shoplifters."

Sam looks around, the atmosphere has gone quiet the entourage look towards him in silence, Alice gives him a side ward glance, and she breaks the silence

"What d'yuh means Sam, about pleasing their superiors? Who are their superiors?"

Sam had to think quick

"Well what I mean is the copper in charge has to take a bollocking for not catching anybody for all the raids that have been going on, just like you Alice, if anything went wrong with the girls I'd imagine you or Albert would have something to say....."

Alice looks straight at him, pauses.

"Well for one thing, I look after my girls, Albert don't have no say in the matter, good, bad, or indifferent."

"okay Alice"

"Right, start up the music again"

The atmosphere changes, the mood of the gathering gets back into full swing.

"Rose could I have a quick word?"

Rose follows Alice into the parlour of the house.

"Close the door – look, I know you're fond of Sam but what do you think about his background an' everything?"

"Well funnily enough I haven't asked him many questions about his past, I thought that if Albert trusts him, I mean he's a pretty good judge of character ain't he?"

"Yuh I suppose you're right, but love's blind Rose, just be careful of what you're getting into"

"Course I will Alice, I'm not stupid"

"Right you go back to the party"

Rose leaves, Alice stays, pondering as she lights a cigarette

"You alright Rose, what's that all about?"

"Nothing, Alice wanted to show me a nice piece of jewellery what she kept back, y'know the spoils of war and everything."

"Right"

A loud cheer broke up the awkwardness of the two: Albert enters with his minders, one who is carrying a crate of champagne.

"Where's our Alice, make a space, get a table"

The crate is placed on the table, the bottles are open, corks whipping up into the air, the gathering all moving forward to fill their glasses. Alice enters the foray

"Alice good news, that little blag was well worth the effort"

They embrace

"Can we talk somewhere?"

"Yuh, let's go out the front, a bit of peace 'n' quiet"

Squeezing through the crowded passage, they emerge on to the front pavement.

"Alice we must have hit 'em on their best day, we nicked twenty five grand not bad for twenty minutes work, what'd yuh think?"

"That's good news Albert"

"How did your girls do, no mishaps I hope?"

"No we all got away safe 'n' sound"

"Good let's let it cool down for a couple of days, we'll have a meet, and have a divvy up of everything; that sound all right with you?"

"That's fine, my girls' all keep a low profile for a while, we had a visit from the ole 'bill earlier, he probably knows it's us, but can't prove anything, don't want to spoil a good thing"

"As always Alice, you make the right suggestion, let's go back in, and enjoy the party"

From across the road, the detectives in their cars are taking notes of all the going and comings of people into Alice's house. After waiting for an hour, Rose and Sam appear in the doorway with drinks, smoking, they start to embrace, Sam turns to a commotion down the street, giving one of the detectives a full frontal vision of Sam.

Sam who sees a movement in the car turns his head quickly away, but not before one of the observers had seen his face: he bends forward to look nose to the windscreen, tapping it with his fingers.

"What's the matter with you? Looks like you spotted Spring-Heeled Jack"

"What's the matter with me? I swear that was one of our faces I've seen down at the station."

"You go back in your seat, we'll give it another ten minutes, an' we'll slope off down the Cut for a nice little night-cap."

Making sure that he kept Rose between him and the car, he manoeuvres rose back into the party, putting his head into her shoulder.

"Oh Sam what's come over you? Don't worry I can take all that 'n' more"

Chapter 6

A DAY LATER ST PANCRAS STATION

Sam, Foden are sitting back to back in the waiting room, Foden has a paper, wide open to hide his face, and to camouflage his speech

"Bloody fine caper that was, they got away with thousands, the "Forty Thieves" clear up as well. Jesus, the place is coming down like a one horse dive"

"I know boss, there was nothing I could do about it, Rose gave all the drivers the information at the last minutes, nobody knew what their right hand was doing.

"Sam we ain't getting no closer to nicking this lot, something's gotta break, you gotta get right into Alice's confidence, an' be quick about it, they'll be bleeding lifting the crown jewels from the Tower of London next"

Sam laughs.

"It ain't funny: we could both be out of a job if we don't get a result, did you see the papers? We must be the laughing stock of the whole of London"

"The thing is guv, I can't put Rose in the frame, she's right close to Alice, she's as sharp as a pin, if she gets the slightest inclination that I'm getting too nosey, the whole thing'll go up the swanny"

"Okay work on it, keep in touch, by the way your other compatriots are getting quite worried about you, you might have to send 'em a get well soon postcard"

He slowly folds his paper walks out of the room, looks positively at his platform ticket, then mingles with the crowds. For his part, Sam walks into the station bar.

The next day Sam and Rose are in a restaurant taking afternoon tea

 "Rose I've been thinking…."

"Now you be careful, you know it doesn't do you any good"

"No seriously, would you like to come round, spend an evening at my place, I'll get some food and wine in, make a nice night of it, we could listen to Henry hall. He has some good guests on sometimes, what'd you think? Nobody to bother us?"

"Well I wonder when you was going to ask me, but could I trust you? I mean you are a young man an' I'm a young lady, suppose you get carried away by the atmosphere of the night"

She puts her head down to tease him.

"Oh no, nothing like that, I'll take you home early, right to your front door...."

"If you do that I won't come round" she teases.

Sam didn't know whether to laugh or cry, she leans over to kiss him

"I can't wait sweetness, I'm counting the minutes"

ALBERT CLUB

Albert is sitting around his regular table, with his lieutenants, Sam is in attendance, the atmosphere is heavy with cigar smoke

"Well boys that was a nice little earner Sidney, bring out the envelopes for the "divvy-up", as you can see you all get the same, so I don't want any aggravation of who's getting what, Sam as you are a new member to our little enterprise, I wanna ask you if you wanna be a full time member, what'd yuh say?"

Sam looks around to the other members of the gang, their faces, expressionless.

"Yuh I'd appreciate that very much, cheers Albert"

"Right a toast to our new member"

Later Sam's drinking with the group, Fred, Albert's number one saunters over to Albert.

"You alright with 'im? There's something I ain't too sure about him, he seems to have slid in to easy, like a snake in the grass"

"What's the matter with you Fred, why you always suspicious of new blood?"

"I dunno, some things don't add up, like how did he know about that dog fight, all prepared then he helps you out?"

"Listen if he hadn't saved me from getting kicked from them pikeys, I'd be in St Thomas's in intensive care, no, I owe him that, you keep an eye on him if it suits yuh, but don't upset things, we got a good thing going with Alice, I don't want it spoilt, you understand.... I said you understand?"

"I'll get in touch with one of my grasses down the nick, see what the full "S.P" is"

"You do that, in the meantime don't cause any grief, go an' have a drink with 'im"

THAT NIGHT: SAM'S FLAT

"How was it coming through the buildings? They can be a bit spooky coming on your own, you should 'ave told me earlier, I could have met you in the courtyard"

"No worry sweetness, Fred brought me to the top of the landing...."

Sam, holding a bottle of wine stops in mid-pouring

"Fred, oh yuh, what did he want?"

"No as soon as I told Alice where I was going she told Albert, Fred insisted, wouldn't let it go, he knew the cab driver would only drop me at the corner, I thought it quite gentlemanly of him, he doesn't usually go out of his way to help anyone"

Sam pauses

"If you say so Rose, what's he like this Fred?"

"What'd mean, he's Albert's right hand man, I would assume to have that position, there ain't no flies on him, Albert recruited him from the "Abbey Street Boys" they never forgot that, there was a couple of attacks on him, he sorted 'em good 'n' proper, razored them up with something terrible, then finished it up with his blackjack, quietened down a bit now, anyway what's all the interest in 'im? I ain't come round to give you his biography"

"No nothing Rose, just that I feel a bit uneasy in his company sometimes"

"Don't worry about it, unless you've got something to hide"

She laughs, looks him straight in the eye "You've got nothing to hide have you Sam?"

"Only this"

He hands her a glass, kisses her hard on the lips. One hour later they are in bed.

"Tell me Rose, why hasn't Alice got herself a man? She had some bad experiences earlier on?"

"Y'know Sam you shouldn't ask sensitive questions like that..... she doesn't confide in me much with personal things, I'll admit though she's got a soft spot for me, but I don't play on it you know what I mean"

"Point taken love, it's just that she's a fascinating woman"

"I'll drink to that"

"Did you tell Fred not to wait, I have booked your company for the night"

"'ark at him"

They both roll over, kissing laughing.

Down below in the courtyard, Fred witnesses the light being turned off, he positions himself in the car seat, pulling a blanket around his shoulders takes a hip flask from his pocket, slowly drinking a large portion of brandy, it was going to be a long night.

FLASHBACK

When she was younger, Alice was badly abused by her boyfriend, she was raped by him and had a daughter that died of T.B. at the age of 3. Heartbroken, she never got involved with a man again. Over the years she hardened to the way of life, becoming more street wise. She adopted Rose from the local orphanage, and over the years they get involved with the "Elephant Gang".

1916 A SLUMHOUSE IN BERMONDSEY

Alice is the second oldest of four children three boys, two girls, her mother takes in washing from all the occupants down the street. Her father was a dispatch rider on the Western Front. The three boys were always in trouble with the police, only one week earlier two of them were put in borstal for stealing fruit off a market stall in East Street. It was not for personal gain but to subsidise the meagre food shortage that family of six had to live on and experience. This led to Alice being looked upon as the bread winner, she was very close to her mother and confided in her with all her thoughts. As her mother suffered from whooping cough, the hard work of handling the washing day after day took a terrible strain on her health, on her fortieth birthday, the dampness of all the washing hanging around her scullery in the kitchen at last took its toll.

One late afternoon, Alice came home to find bags of washing in the passage; this was out of character for Lillian, as she was always prompt to make sure that the washing had to be kept up to date to return to customers on specific times.

"Mum where are you?"

Her two sisters came out of the front crying

"What's the matter girls, where's mum?"

Through sobs and tears, one of the two older girls choked back her explanation.

"Mum's not well, the doctor came round, he's upstairs with her now"

Alice doesn't want hear more. Dropping her bags, she rushes upstairs to catch the doctor on the landing just about to close his doctors bag

"Doctor what's the matter with mum?"

The bedroom door is slightly ajar, the doctor pulls his hand to his lips, gesturing her to keep quiet

"Let's go downstairs."

He follows Alice into the scullery, moving the wet washing

"Your mother has chronic asthma with a whooping cough" he points to all the washing around the room

"All the paraphernalia has got to go; your mother's days of a washer woman are over, I want all these items taken down, returned to their respective owners without delay."

He gets out his prescription pad, jots down the information

"I'll write out this prescription, you can pick it up from me at the surgery first thing in the morning"

He hands her the note

"Now remember get rid of all this damp washing straight away"

He turns to leave.

"Doctor I'm not working, how can I afford the medicine, dad's in the war, we ain't got no money coming into the house if we give this up"

The doctor pauses

"I'm sorry, there's nothing else I can do. Put on a course of this medicine for a week, then see how she reacts to the procedure. If there is no improvement by the end of the week I'll make arrangements to have her put in hospital. I'm very sorry, but that's all I can do."

He made his way past the two crying younger sisters, patting them on the head.

Alice enters the bedroom, her mother is propped up against the pillows, she is a jaundiced looking person, she forces a half hearted strained smile.

"How you feeling mum?"

Alice holds back her tears, gets on the bed, laying with her, starts to stroke Alice's hair, her voice is very low keyed, she starts to talk but a bout of coughing takes over.

"Alice promise me you'll take care of the babies until I get better, then maybe I'll look for something better, this will be over in a couple of months, dad'll be home, an' we'll be a family again."

She starts to cough, which turns into a croaking noise, the younger girls peak from behind a half closed door

"Come in girls, jump up on the bed, give mum a big cuddle like we all used to do"

The girls jump up on the other side of the bed, crying

"What's all that for, get your pecks up, I'll be alright."

They all cuddle together, the girls crying, Alice holds back her tears, thinking of the repercussions with no money coming into the house.

NEXT DAY SATURDAY MORNING EARLY

Alice, the girls, were bagging up all the washing, it was still damp, the dried washing waiting to go to the customers, was in a neat row in the passage.

"Right girls get the pram out of the front room, you're gonna help your mother a lot more from now on, we're going to collect her wages for this lot, then it's all over, we gotta find a new way to make a living, alright?"

The girls laughed, they didn't realise the seriousness of the situation. Outside in the street the pram was fully loaded with the bags of washing, Alice pushed, while the two girls pulled a rope attached to the axle laughing. It was a hard slog, over the uneven pavements, cobbled roads, it would have been a hard job for a male, but it was a mammoth task for the girls.

At each house she had to explain the situation that this would be the last time of washing, explaining the predicament, all of the loyal customers gave her an extra six pence. At the last house they sat down on the kerbstone, eating some buns out of the extra money.

"Alice, what are we gonna do with the pram?" Sally asked, Alice pauses, smiles, looks up and down the street

"Well you know that old costermonger round the corner, go and ask her if she wants it"

They run down the street laughing, disappearing around the corner, two minutes later they return, still laughing

"What'd she say?"

"Yes, but she ain't gonna pay yuh"

"I didn't expect her to"

They push the pram eating their buns to the corner, there is a slight incline to the road, leading to the front façade of the shop with all the junk displayed

"Now girls you go back an' wait for me around the corner"

Alice waits until they disappear, she directs the pram straight in line to the shop, with a loud whistle, she hails the shop owner, she slowly appears in the doorway looking up and down the street, Alice whistles again, the costermonger focuses dead ahead, Alice pulls back the pram, then pushes it as hard as she could, to send it careering down the shop front, the owner could not believe her eyes, only at the last minute did she vacate her stance, jumping back into the safety of the shop, the pram went flying into her display, cascading the goods all over the pavement, Alice takes one last look, runs but finding it hard as she cannot stop laughing. Out of eyesight and earshot she collects the girls, they are all laughing, making their escape up the street, out of sight of Alice, a man is reading a paper at a coffer stall, folding the paper, keeping his distance, he follows Alice to her house.

LATER THAT MORNING

With the money that she had collected from her customers, she goes to the doctors surgery to pick up the prescription

"This course will last for one week, I'll come round to see your mother if there is no improvement, she'll have to go into hospital; I'm sorry to say but there would be a change at the end of the treatment, would you be able to meet the criteria?"

"I'll have to find the money somehow doctor, but the most important thing is to get mum well by your next visit"

"I understand, your mother has always been a hard working member of the community, I delivered the two little girls-"

Alice could not restrain her emotions anymore; she burst into tears, running out of the surgery, much to the peoples concern, waiting in the room adjacent to the surgery.

6 OCLOCK THAT NIGHT

Alice is in her mother's bedroom holding a cold flannel over her mother's head, the children are downstairs playing with their makeshift dolls, a knock on the door stops their playing, Alice looks to her mum.

"Who could that be Alice, are you expecting anybody?"

"No mum, girls don't open the door"

Alice adjusts her dress to look presentable, slowly walking down the stairs.

"Go into the parlour girls, shut the door behind you"

The girls pick up their dolls, duly go as told, giggling.

Alice takes a deep breath, opens the door halfway.

It was the man who was taken an interest in her earlier on; he was dark, swarthy and smart with a small bowler hat, which he takes off, softly spoken.

"I'm sorry to bother you at this time unannounced, could I have a quick word with you?"

Alice, being street wise, holds the door firmly, her foot tightly wedged at the bottom of the door so that it couldn't be forced back,

"What's your business?" She replied arrogantly

"Well I noticed earlier on today you were with your sisters I take it?"

"Carry on"

"Well I couldn't help but notice how well behaved they were, and you pushing that heavy pram, and I got to thinking that you might be open to a proposition I'm going to make to you"

Alice is getting a bit nervous, but holds her grounds

"What it is I'm involved, a spokesman if you like for a little club, it's like a bring and buy club with owing money to the tally man, you wouldn't have to do anything illegal, just to keep tabs on the books, what'd you think..... you'd get a regular wage, and if you fancy anything for the kids or the family you'd get a good discount, and with Christmas coming on it could be right handy for you..... well what'd you think, I don't know what your personal financial situation is but we could all do with the little extras couldn't we?"

Alice had to think quick, but before she could give a positive or negative answer

"Listen, what's your name by the way?"

"Rose"

"Nice name, my mother was called that, if you're interested pop in the "Eagle" tomorrow night, six o'clock, ask for Conny. Everybody knows me, think about it...."

He looks her straight in the eye, produces five one pound notes.

"Take this, buy the kids something for your trouble"

Rose slowly holds out her hand, what had she got to lose? She couldn't pluck up the courage to thank him.

He turns to go but stalls, smiling.

"By the way, that was right funny what you done with the pram, a crowd gathered after you two a toast down the road, nobody liked the old bag, made my day, see you later Rose."

Rose did not answer, closing the door with her back she says there, pondering what her next move would be, and looking at the money in her hand she raises it to her mouth, slowly smiling

"Yes I'll think about it, you bet I will"

A call from the children breaks her concentration.

"Can we come out now Rose?"

"Course you can my little angels"

Rose goes back up to her mother, continues to bather her head.

"Who was that luv?"

"Oh the followers from down the mission asking if I had any lose change for the brethren. I told 'em if I had any, it wouldn't be for the brethren"

They both laughed.

The next day, Rose and the children went down the market, Rose was in a jubilant mood, she had never experienced having the money to spend on anything the children wanted, it got her thinking she would go to the "Eagle", just for the hell of it

Stopping by a toy stall, the children stepped and stared, Rose kept up the impasse, the children in complete silence, not daring to touch the toys

"Come on girls we can't afford those"

The girls walk away, taking a long lingering look at the untouchable toys. She bends down pulls them close together whispering in their ears.

"Yes we can"

The smiles return to their forlorn faces as they run back to the stall.

"Choose anything you want"

Slowly the children look at the toys, then the vendor, they pick what they wanted, then saunter down the market. Rose stops at the poultry stall to buy a chicken, moving on to a vegetable stall, to get enough for two or three days. Finishing up at the bakers, she buys the girls two large cream cakes, they end up at the local park, where they spend what was left of the morning playing on the swings.

Rose sits on the pink bench, pondering what it would be like to be in this position all the time.

When at last they got home, Rose went straight upstairs her mother was fast asleep, Rose starts to sob, holding back the tears, leaves the room.

After an hour her mother calls out, Rose goes up to ask her if she wants a tea or coffee.

"Are you joking Rose, we ain't had coffee since the beginning of the war"

"Don't worry mum I'll bring you up a nice cup of coffee and a salt beef sandwich, with mustard"

Rose is laying beside her mum

"That was lovely Rose, where'd you get the money for that?"

"Don't worry mum, none of it came out of the bag wash float, I found a purse down the market, I know what you're gonna say, I should've taken it round to the station, but they always tell you someone claimed it, you know full well they'd dip it, what can you say?"

Her mother didn't answer.

SUNDAY NIGHT – 7 OCLOCK

Alice was in front of the living room mirror, putting the last of her makeup on that she had brought from the gift, the two girls were looking up in awe of their big sister, she turns and smiles, puts a little bit of rough on their cheeks, they giggle, then look in the mirror, Alice goes upstairs to see her mother

"Alice you look lovely, don't be late home, an' keep together with your friends, if I'm asleep when you come back home, tell me about the film in the morning"

She kisses her mother, telling the sisters to behave themselves and go to bed at the right time, not to wake her mother

Alice was full of trepidation on her journey up to the "Eagle", wondering if she made the right decision, on arrival at the door of the saloon bar, she pauses, people push past her to get in, and punters leaving, her confidence leaves her, she decides to go home, turns, at that moment her would be suitor caught a glimpse of her through the open doorway, it was this encounter that was to change her life forever.

"Alice hang about – where you going?"

She turns, forcing a smile

"You look nice girl, come inside, I want you to meet some people"

Alice is overawed by the whole experience, she is invited to sit round a table, taking stock of her surroundings, she's quickly at the young age of the female company, after being introduced to them, and their male counterparts leans over to her

"Come over to the bar, we'll get a drink there"

The punters in the bar look over the top of their glasses, or put them down to acknowledge the new comer, one of Conny's friends whisper in his ear while at the bar

"You got a right Solomon there, Conny"

He smiles to himself

"Hope so"

Alice, sitting at the table looks round to see smiling admiring faces looking at her, it wasn't long till her confidence returned, after an hour of small talk, he slowly brought into the conversation about what he wanted to offer Alice.

"Well Alice I don't know what you're doing at the moment but what I'm involved with is like a bring an' buy sale, you know like if you buy something say like a dress in shop an' it don't fit right when you get home, you take it back, well sometimes one of the girls forgets to pay for the garment, so not to be lumbered with it, she returns it and gets the money in return, everybody's happy, y'know what I mean?"

Alice is taken aback a bit.

"But what about the receipt, don't they ever ask for it?"

"Clever girl, yes they do, but they just say they've lost it, it's a little bit hooky, but the big stores can afford it."

Alice is pondering over the situation, wondering where this line of conversation was going, it wasn't long before she found out.

"Well what I'm thinking, mind you, you don't have to make a decision tonight, if you would be interested in making a little bit of pocket money on side, it's gotta beat taking in washing, you could buy your little sisters some toys, look after your mum a bit better....."

Alice stops him mid sentence

"How d'you know about my mum an' sisters?"

"Sorry Alice, don't get me wrong, y'know what it's like round 'ere, everybody knows each other business, it ain't such a bad thing sometimes, like now for example, we can both help each other out"

"So let's get to the point, what d'you want me to do?"

"That's better Alice, well what I was going to suggest that you have a little visit with a couple of the girls on their next survey just to see if you like it, if you don't, fair enough, no love lost"

Alice runs her finger round the top of the glass, looking round at the girls on the other tables, they are a couple of years older than her, but she is taken in by their fine clothes, how much they're enjoying themselves

"When d'yuh want to know the answers?"

"Soon as poss."

Alice empties her glass in one mouthful.

"Okay I'm in, the Provo being that if I don't like it after the first job, I can walk away, no love lost, no hard feelings, ok?"

"That's what I like to hear Alice, straight to the point, no love lost, I like that, right now I'd like to introduce you to the girls proper"

Alice was to spend another two hours with her newfound accomplices, getting up to go home she was a bit unsteady on her feet, as she straightened up to her full height, the girls laughed.

"Right Alice I think I better walk you to the corner"

"Okay but only to the corner"

More laughter.

On the short journey to her house Rose starts to sober up, as was arranged they stop at the corner.

"Right Alice I won't ask if I can come in, 'cos I know the answer right? What I would like to say is you could meet two of the girls on the corner of East Street Market Tuesday morning, they'll show you the ropes"

Alice is in a bit of a quandary; she liked his self confidence but didn't want to show her feelings on the first meeting

He made a move to embrace her, she declines

"Easy tiger, it's only the first night"

He laughs, not taking the advantage, he holds out his hand as if in a good will gesture, Rose takes up the invitation not knowing why, on letting go, her palm is left holding several notes, he walks away, turning.

"Get yourself a new dress, look smart, night Alice"

It wasn't until she was in the passage of her house she looked to see what he gave her, it was three five pound notes, she gasps puts her hand to her mouth, it was only the belated call of her mother that brought her back to her senses.

"Coming mum"

She firstly looks into the girls room, they are both asleep clutching their new toys, Alice pauses, taking in their angelic innocent faces, a lump goes into her throat, she quietly closes the door.

"It's a bit late Rose, what was the film like?"

Rose props up her pillow.

"It was good, we started to watch the second performance but 'alf way through they cottoned on, we 'at to leave, that Fred Astaire, Ginger Rogers, can they dance, anyway, how you feeling?"

"Well that jollop you got seems to be relaxing me chest a little better, only thing is when it runs out, where we gonna get the money for some more, an' food for all us?"

She starts to cry, Alice holds her hand, puts the damp flannel across her forehead, looks away, gets up to turn the blanket above her chest.

"Don't worry mum, something a' turn up."

Alice was up early the next day, after seeing to the children, she told her mother that she was going to look at the new store that had opened down at the "Elephant". Her first port of call was the market, she wanted to break into one of the fivers just in case she might lose it, she brought some vegetables, fruit cakes for the girls, then some chops, the person behind the counter gave her an old fashioned look as she passed it over, he held it up to the light to scrutinise it, not satisfied, he called over one of his staff, they both look at it again, satisfied

"You can't be too careful these days, what with all these foreigners bringing over counterfeit money"

After making her way through the market she ends up at the new store, going straight to the ladies fashion department, she picks out a smart dress, to finish off with a French beret. As she is looking at herself in the full length mirror, she sees the reflection of men looking in the mirror at her, she turns, she smiles, the man embarrassed walks away, then turns back for a second glance: Alice had arrived; expectations, and the outlook for Alice would never be the same again. On the way, she purchased a pair of shoes, gloves, handbag

On opening her front door, the house was quiet, the girls were out, slowly going up the stairs to her room she quietly hangs the dress on a hanger, hiding the other items on the top shelf of the wardrobe, pushing them to the back then covering them with some old clothes, she looks around the half opened door of her mother's room, she is asleep, looking very pale

Alice in the kitchen is preparing a meal. When there is a knock on the door, it was the children returning from the child minder.

They push past her to go into the scullery for their toys but noticing the unopened bags on the table retrieve the cakes out of the bag

"That's a nice smell Alice, what you cooking?"

"Oh some old tripe 'n' onions"

"Save some for me, see you tomorrow"

"Come away from them bags, they're for after dinner"

The girls laugh, surrendering the contents to Alice.

The meal was a great success, the children were full up, forgetting about the cakes; Alice had made a meal for her mother which she took up.

"Her mother finished off the meal in silence

"That was lovely Alice, where you'd get the money for it?"

"Well I've been offered a little job, but I took a little advance, treat ourselves."

"What little job?"

"Oh y'know, it's like the tally man, but different, the girls supply me with dresses, clothes, y'know that sort of thing. I sell them for a little bit of profit, and keep the rest, it comes at just the time. Strange innit, that's fate for you."

Her mother starts to cough again, Alice givers her a glass of water

That night, with the girls in bed, Alice retrieves the clothes from the cupboard, slowly puts them on, looks in the mirror, and parades around the room, she feels that this is the direction she wants to pursue.

Chapter 7

INSIDE THE EAGLE: NEXT DAY

The meeting came up to Alice's expectations, the girls were dressed very smart, she had brought her dress, accessories to change in the back room; when she came out, the girl looked at her, there was a deep silence, and she was transformed into a different person. Alice was embarrassed, more so when she saw Conny looking at her, smiling, slowly nodding his head.

"Right girls let's get the show on the road; Lillian I want you to take Alice under your wing, Patsy, Linda, you start up front, don't take any unnecessary risk remember we've got a new girl in training, don't want to scare her off on her first introduction do we now Okay here's your float....."

He hands each girl ten pounds

"I don't expect to get t all back but make it worth your while"

The girls finish off their chats, pick up their large carpet bags, one is handed to Alice.

"Just in case we get overloaded"

TWO HOURS LATER; REGENT STREET

"Now Alice you just stay close to me, don't look surprised at anything you see, the name of the game is confidence, anybody gives you a tug look, look 'em straight in the eye, deny everything"

Alice nods her head

Once inside the store, Lillian lets Patsy and Linda walk two yards in front until they stop at a chosen counter, this time, it was to be silk scarves, gloves, imitation jewellery, Lillian stops at the same counter, puts her bag next to Linda, what happened next was so fast Alice couldn't believe it, Patsy reached over to a display item of gloves, remove them from the pedestal, while Linda covered her arm, she drops the item into the bag on the floor, Patsy now with the imitation jewellery stands back to admire herself, the counter assistant comes up.

"Can I help madam? We do have a further collection in our display cabinet"

"That would be very nice, are these from the Continent? They seem very fashionable."

"Yes madam"

She bends down to retrieve a further collection, placing them on the velvet pad on top of the counter.

"Would madam like to try them on?"

"Thank you"

While the counter assistants attention is being taken up Lillian gets hold of Rose's elbow, gently manipulating so that she becomes a barrier between the counter assistant, she reaches over the counter to take several silk scarves off a mannequins neck, slides them into her bag, pulls Rose to her, gastrulates with her head to move slowly off to the lift, to go to the next level of the store.

This takes them to the dress department; Lillian proceeds to sit down on a large round leather seat, Alice props herself next to her.

"Well Rose what'd think of our little enterprise?"

Alice is trembling.

"I'll be honest with you, I'm bloody scared but at the same time fascinated to what I had just witnessed"

Lillian laughs.

"That's nothing; you wait till we get started, just watch and learn; now you see it, now you don't"

Five minutes later the other duo enter the room, they totally ignore Lillian and Rose, go over to a dress rail, slowly pushing the dresses back, Linda holds ne up to her body, slowly manoeuvring herself in front of the large tall standing mannequin to witness Lillian going into one of the changing cubicles; Patsy has got the attention of the assistant, manoeuvring her so that she is in the opposite direction of Lillian's departure. An entrance inside the changing room, where she gets up onto the ledge, she bends down, half opens the door, so as not to draw attention to make it look like its vacant. Alice is speechless, she is still sitting on the leather seat, amazed at the speed that Lillian had disappeared so quickly, looking round pensively, common sense told her to keep from panicking after all, the girls had done this so many times before it was common practice

"What d'you think of this, does it suit me?"

"Yes madam"

"Does it go with my complexion?"

"We do have some others in a different shade"

She turns to walk across the room to retrieve another dress, Linda with her back to the assistant, is now concealed by Lillian who walks round to the other side of the dress rack, Patsy quickly pushes four of the dresses to the end of the rack, expertly takes them off the rack, folds them into a square, pulling the other dresses along to take up the now vacant space, she puts them into her carpet bag slowly walks away to another part of the room

"Would madam like this one?"

Linda ponders, on the other side of the room there is a commotion, the assistant looks around to witness Patsy toppling over with the mannequin underneath her, the assistant rushes over; this was Linda's' opportunity from a different rack, she lifts four dresses, walks calmly into the changing room where Lillian is crouched on the wooden ledge, passes them to her, she folds them puts them into her bag then quite casually goes back to sit with Alice, getting Patsy out of her dilemma, the assistant walks back to Linda

"I'm sorry about that madam, but the poor lady had an altercation with one of our mannequins, she's quite upset."

"Yes I can see, poor woman, I don't think these dresses are what I'm quite looking for, thank you for your help"

Linda composes herself walks out of the room, Patsy follows just a few minutes later Alice and Lillian leave the room leading to the shoe department, Alice is now getting over the initial shock of the way the girls manipulated the situation to suit themselves, the adrenaline was starting to work, waiting what was to be the next escapade. It was not long in waiting. Patsy and Linda took up positions in a row of chairs, with their backs to one another

"Alice you go over to the counter, just watch like before"

Lillian casually takes her place with a two gap space next to Linda. There is a collection in front of the two, an assistant comes over.

"Has madam seen anything she likes?"

Lillian points to a pair of shoes

"Certainly madam, what size?"

"Seven"

"Yes we have that one in stock"

"Do you have it with the kitten heal?"

"I'll have a look"

Linda for her part is looking at the display in front of her

"Excuse me, when your ready could you help me please?"

The assistant is distracted, this was the first part of the operation to get the assistant flustered, then to push home the advantage.

Patsy has got another assistant to bring her different styles of shoes, in a few minutes she has five different pairs slowly parading up and down to stop to look into the mirror, not satisfied with a pair she sits down, turns to open her bag, on the other side of the row of chairs, Lillian is using a shoe to put a pair on, with also a large selection in front of her, the assistant walks away, this was the gambit for Patsy, Lillian quickly pushes two pairs of shoes to Patsy under the chairs, her assistant has been asked if she would try them on, turns to walk away Patsy puts the manoeuvred shoes from Lillian into her bag, covering them with a scarf.

"I think there a bit on the low side, and the toe is not round enough, I'll leave it for today, thank you"

"Yes madam"

Patsy got up to leave; on her way she moves her eye in a movement for Alice to follow her.

Lillian is shaking her head.

"It's not quite what I was looking for, the shade is not one or another"

"Would madam like to look at our French collection? They only arrived yesterday."

"Oh no I'm fine with continental shoes thank you"

Putting her own shoes back on, she looks across to Linda winks at her, Linda walks off, Lillian slowly puts on her coat, walks slowly off, takes one last look at the melee they had left behind, it looked like somebody had emptied a large part of the shoe department leaving it in total disarray.

The girls next met up in the tea room, ordering the beverages cake, they planned their next escapade.

"Right girls I think our next port of call will be the cosmetic department, Alice you could become an important part of our assistance, when we go in, they pounce on you like bees on a 'honey pot, you just hold the attention of one of them for start, we'll work out how we can off load some smellies and foundation cream."

Lillian laughs.

On entering the perfumery department Lillian guides Alice to an assistant with a customer, Alice sits down patiently waiting to be attended to, this was good, as it allowed the assistant to be busy; Alice by now is getting quietly confident waiting for her turn to be made up or manicured.

The two now slipped into their well-rehearsed operation, Lillian and Patsy approach who they have decided suspected of being the most vulnerable assistant, Patsy starts to ask questions about the products, takes her coat off to put the woman at ease, looks into the mirror for the consultation to begin, Lillian for her part looks on approvingly agreeing with all what the women suggest getting behind her, she slips for of the expensive perfumes into her bag keeping her body between the counter and the walkway, putting the bag on the floor, Linda walks by, exchanges her bag for Lillian's, walks casually off towards Alice once again with the eye movement, Alice slowly gets up to follow her, keeping several paces behind her she catches up with her in the evening wear department, where they sit together on leather settee. An assistant comes over to ask them if they need any help.

"Well what'd you think of your first day – enjoy it?"

"Well it was a bit scary at first, I thought you were going to get caught, then I realized how professional you were I quite enjoyed it really."

"The truth is Alice always remember, not to be greedy, quit while you're in front, I think Conny'll be pleased with your performance today, we'll just wait for the girls, see if everything is alright."

They didn't have to wait long, the duo appeared Patsy has her makeover done, smiling.

They leave.

THE EAGLE: TWO HOURS LATER.

The four girls are in the back room with Conny, the atmosphere is heavy with smoke, Alice is careful with her drink, after all she has to get back home sober, she just gets offered a weak shandy, the stolen items are paraded on a table in the middle of the room, Conny slowly goes through them, appraising them as he does.

"You know girls, you done very well today."

We'll give it a miss tomorrow, let the other girls have a go, keep it fresh... well Alice, how did you find your first experience, did you enjoy yourself:-wanna do it again?"

He looks round to the girls, they echo his laugh,

"Well Conny, it was a bit scary at first, I was ready to do a runner in the ladies dress department but I forced myself in the sea, I had to keep turning away like a bleeding ventriloquist dummy every time the assistant caught my eye."

They laugh.

"Never mind, what I'd like to do, if the girls are in agreement mind, as it was your first introduction to our hopefully ongoing business venture, I think it would be in order to let you choose one dress, and a pair of shoes to your liking what'd you think girls?"

It was a chorus of one, they cheered and laughed. Alice was overcome with emotion, she started to cry, it went silent; Patsy was the first to bring over a short;

"Ere you are Alice, get that down yeh make you feel better."

Alice drinks it in one gulp, chokes and laughs, the entourage joining in with her, Alice slowly goes along the table, then stops to pick out her dress, then the shoes, puts the dress up to her torso, the girls clap in admiration, then the shoes.

"Give us the dress 'ere a minute Alice."

Lillian form her bag produces a small pair of tailors scissors, proceeds to cut the clothe carefully around the label, put it into her hand, shows it to Alice then puts it in her mouth, Alice is dumfounded, Lillian opens her mouth, its empty, shows Alice her hands, there empty, Alice sees the joke - they all laugh.

"Remember Alice, the movement defies the yes, always get rid of the evidence as quick as you can."

"Okay girls wrap it up, Alice you'd better start to make your way home."

Alice carefully folds the dress into her bag, Walks to the exit of the pub, Conny follows.

"Well Alice I'd like you to join the team, you think it over for a couple of days pop into see only just keep schtum about everything else."

She walks two steps, turns.

"I don't have to think it over Conny, I'd love to join see you in a couple of days."

Conny smiles.

On arrival at her front door Alice has an extra bah with some food and sweets for the kids. She quietly lets herself in, bypassing the scullery door where the children are playing behind, reaching the landing, her mother's voice, breaks her concentration.

"That you Alice dear?"

"Yes Mum."

"It's pretty late, where you bin, you alright?"

"Yuh, don't worry Mum, you been taking your medicine, you been eating alright?"

"Yuh I finished off that chick soup, cant swallow proper with this bloody cough."

"Right I'll be there in just a minute, take m' coat off."

In her bedroom she dutifully takes of her coat, takes the new dress out, puts it up against herself, puts on the shoes, the children are laughing, clambering up the stairs Alice breaks her composure, she quickly puts it on a hanger, pushing to the end of the rail, bringing her older clothes up to conceal it, the shoes are hurriedly put under some old bags, the kids come into the room she hugs them.

"I've got something for you girls."

From her bag she retrieves some sweets and small oranges.

"Now you go down and play for a little while, I'm just gonna see mum, then I'll cook your tea."

They run off giggling.

Alice is sitting on the end of the bed, her mother propped up, she is not looking well, grey, thin.

"Mum I gonna see the doctor tomorrow, see if he can put you in one them convalescent homes only for a short time, just to get you on your feet."

"No Alice, I can't do that, what about the children 'an yourself?"

"Mum don't worry, only for a couple of weeks till you get better, the worse be' over, Dad'll be 'ome, what I would like to do is to take the girls to Aunt Nora while your away, I could visit them, keep an eye on 'em, 'an visit you in between."

"When did these arrangements come into your head then?"

"I've been thinking about it for a long time, with the winter coming on 'n that, with your cough, a damp house ain't gonna make it any better.

Her mother goes silent, she could understand the reasoning.

Alice true to her word arranged for the doctor to visit her mum. After examining her he agrees with Alice that she would have a spell in the Sanatorium in the country, he would make the arrangements for the admission but Alice would have to organize the transportation, Alice agreed. She would visit him at the end of the week.

Alice went up to her room but the news was greeted in silence, The next job was to go an visit her Aunt Nora to arrange the accommodation for the girls.

When she saw them later, they took the news in good spirits, it was just another holiday to them.

The next morning Alice was tidying up her mums bedroom,

"Alice, how'd you get on with the clothes?"

Alice who is bending down, cleaning under the bed, stops in her tracks – pauses.

"Not too bad, some of the women paid cash but most of them brought 'em on the cheap."

"Well I don't suppose any of them can go up to the West End 'an buy 'em for cash off the 'anger."

Alice relaxes, smiles and laughs.

"Now that would be lovely if any of us could do that."

From behind the door, the giggling of the children broke the conversation; they both look quizzical at the door.

"What are those little angels up to?"

Mother queries:

Seconds later the girls burst into the room, Alice is open mouthed, annoyed at first, her mother cannot believe her eyes, the girls are all dressed up in Alice's dresses, as they come in, they trip over Alice's shoes, with the long gloves going up to the top of their arms, her mother could do nothing but start laughing amongst her coughing the children look angelic, humour gets the better of Alice, she laughs and goes to cuddle the children for a few seconds, this was to be rudely stopped by her mother's breathing into her wretched incessant cough, the girls go quiet Alice looks around, her mother's pyjama top is covered in blood, Alice acted fast, turning the children's head she ushers them out of the bedroom, Alice threw her arms around their shoulders, the peep round, two witness the last time they would see their mother.

"Now you be good girls, go downstairs, play in the dresses I'll just go 'an see Mum, be down in a minute, take the shoes off."

In one long stride she was across the bedroom her mother was looking terrible, scared.

"Oh mum darling let me clean you up luv."

Alice props her back up, she was all skin and bones with no weight, after propping her up, cleaning her, she gives her a glass of water mother looks into Alice's eyes.

"Promise me you'll look after the girls Alice."

Alice smiles trying to put on a brave face.

"Don't talk like that mum, I'll get the doctor round first thing in the morning, Hell know what to do, I'll put the girls to bed 'an I'll sleep in 'ere tonight."

"You don't have to Alice."

"I do 'ave to mum, now you try 'n get some shut eye."

After settling the girls down for the night, but not before she had to answer their questions as best she could what was the matter with her mum, Alice was very condescending, the children very quiet, Alice goes upstairs to lay down by her mother, who was in a half limbo sleep, every now and again being intercepted by a raucous cough, Alice wiping the blood from her lips. She didn't get much sleep that night, gazing at the ceiling, pondering where her life was going to take her.

Early the next morning Alice takes the girls into a neighbour while she rushes round to the surgery to be first to make an appointment with the doctor.

He told her he would come round as soon as he finished his morning surgery, Alice impressing on the seriousness urgency of her mother's dilemma.

Getting home as quick as she could, she rushes upstairs to her mother, breathing a sigh of relief she is still in a labouring doze, she gently wipes the blood from her lips.

Downstairs she starts to tidy up the kitchen, the girls who had unceremoniously chucked the dresses over the back of the chairs, were studiously slowly picked up by Alice placing them on hangers, picks up the shoes reminiscing laughing at the memory of her sisters dressed up as little girls do, the novelty not lost in their innocence.

Two hours later a knock on the door signalled the doctors visit. In a low tone he asks where her mother was, Alice points up the stairs, the doctor follows to the bedroom door, Alice acts to enter, the doctor nods his head no, Alice duly goes into her bedroom waiting for the visit to end. It was long coming, putting on his coat his instruments in his bag, Alice could tell by the grave look on his face the news wasn't welcome.

"I'm afraid Alice your mother has consumption. The only thing I can recommend is that we get her into a sanatorium as quickly as possible, Do you have the means to pay for the journey and treatment?"

Alice pauses "Yes doctor I can manage that."

"Okay good, time is of the essence, if you could come round tomorrow, with the deposit of five pounds we could have her in the next day, she is pretty bad shape y'know."

Alice nods her head, closing the door behind him she holds her back against it, holding back any loud noise, she sobs hard to herself, stifling the noise with her handkerchief.

Going up to see her mother, she is awake, gives her a glass of water.

"Well mum, the doctor told me you've got to get help as soon as possible, I'll organise everything..."

"What about the girls, where's the money coming from to pay for the medicine 'an treatment?..."

"Don't worry mum I'm organising it, the girls can go round Aunt Nora's for a while, they really love it round there an' she loves the little devils to pieces."

"Alice you make it sound so easy."

"It is mum, don't worry, I'm going out for a little while just to organise some arrangements, you be alright?"

She nods yes, Alice kisses her head.

Going outside the front door, breath out hard, bits her lip she decided quickly what her next course of action was to be.

ENTERING THE 'EAGLE' ONE O'CLOCK

At this time of the day the pub was filled with all kinds of different clientele, from across the bar she could see most of the girls she had been working with earlier, Patsy catches her eye, beckons her over.

"And what do we owe this pleasure Alice luv? We ain't working today, enjoying the spoils."

"Well it is pretty urgent, I gotta see Conny, is he about?"

"Er, well Alice he's in the back room, talking business 'an he don't like to be disturbed like..."

"It is important Patsy."

"Okay, I'll see what I can do."

She walks over – knocks, enters: Inside, Conny, with four other men are sitting round a table playing cards, Conny beckons her over, she whispers in his ear, to her surprise he has her complete attention.

"Gentlemen deal me in/out?"

They duly respond.

"Blimey Conny you onto a promise?"

"You never know."

Putting on his jacket hen quickly walks out the room, glances round to see Alice standing at the end of the bar.

"Hello Alice."

He gently kisses her on the cheek.

"What's going on luv, everything alright?"

She starts to cry.

"Now, now luv, enough of that, come in sit down."

The other girls are taking the situation all in, without speaking. He brings over two glasses of gin.

"Take a sip, now tell me slowly all about it."

Alice proceeds to tell him about the morning's proceedings.

Conny listens intently, not interrupting once, at the end of the conversation, Alice starts to sob again, he gallantly wipes her eyes through her sniffles, she pauses.

"What I would like Conny if I could borrow some money off you just to get the thing moving, get her in as quickly as possible, I could start to work for you as soon as you like. You can have all the money out of my take."

Conny pauses, takes a drink, smiles.

"Now Alice I know the predicament you're in, I'll give you the money, take it as a long term investment, pay it back when you can, no strings, how's that sound?"

Alice starts to sob again.

"Conny I don't know how to thank you."

"Don't."

From his wallet he counts out one hundred pounds and hands it to her.

"When that runs out tell me, now go home sort out your mum, organise the children, come back 'an see me when everything quietened down, ok? Right I gotta get back to card game, you take care."

He kisses her on the cheek, she leaves.

The whole incident didn't not go unnoticed by the girls on the table, they carry on with their gossip, Conny comes over smiling, bends down amongst them.

"Now don't any of you get any funny ideas about it, I got nothing to explain, it's purely business."

Gives Patsy a mock kiss on the lips.

EARLY NEXT MORNING: ALICES HOUSE

Alice is bending down, just finishing doing the button up on the girls coats, they have a few bags with several toys in they are excited, happy but Alice is holding back the tears.

"Right you go up to mum, give big kisses and hugs but don't squeeze her too hard, she not very well at the moment."

They run up the stairs giggling, running into the bedroom jumping up on it, forgetting not to embrace their mother too hard, she starts to cough, but puts her handkerchief up to her mouth just in time to stop the show of blood, as not to scare the children.

"Now you be good girls for Aunt Nora, don't play her up, I'll see you in a couple of weeks when I'm better to come home from the hospital."

They all have a final embrace, they run out of the room excited, laughing:- their mother starts to cough uncontrollably, Alice runs up the stairs.

"Oh mum I'm sorry they squeezed you so much."

"Don't worry Alice luv, it was worth it."

A knock on the door.

"That'll be Aunt Nora, I just let her in."

On opening the door a middle ages lady is in the doorway, the children greet her, holding her around the waist.

"Careful girls, you'll break my bleeding back."

She bends down to kiss them.

"Will it be alright if I just pop up and see her?"

"Yuh but don't ask her too many question's, she's in a bad way."

After several minutes, Nora slowly comes down the stairs, her face is crestfallen, looks Alice in the eye, the both embrace one another, whispering

"Alice love, if you need anything, any problems get in touch with me straight away, I'm always there."

"I know that Aunt Nora, look after the girls, soon as Mums in the hospital I'll come round and visit, I'll have some money…"

"Don't be silly, you look after Mum."

She gives the girls a final hug, they leave, and she goes into the scullery, closes the door sits down to sob uncontrollably.

LATER THAT AFTERNOON: DOCTORS SURGERY

Alice is in conversation with the doctor.

"The transport will be around at six o'clock, have as many changes of clothes, underwear as possible, the place I've organised for her is a sanatorium down in surrey, shell get the best treatment: I'm sorry Alice to be broach a delicate subject but when I mentioned about the finance these people would like a cash advance up front…"

"Of course Doctor."

She reaches into her handbag to give him fifty pounds in notes, He looks at her questionably; she looks back at him in silence, then reading the significance of the situation, forces a smile.

"Oh its nothing like that doctor, I've borrowed the money from family and friends."

"Oh no I didn't mean nothing like that."

At six o'clock the transport duly arrived, her mother is quietly carefully lifted into the transport; once inside lying down, Alice goes into give her a last kiss.

"I'll be down in a weeks' time mum, take care, week soon 'av you 'ome."

She leaves and the transport pulls away, Alice slowly goes inside, sits down to cry again, after an interval she foes up to her mother's room to retrieve the blood stained bed linen stripping the bed, finishing the chores she goes into her bedroom gets out the dresses and shoes, looks at them sobbing and chucks them across the room, thinking they didn't matter one bit.

TWO DAYS LATER: MORNING INSIDE THE EAGLE

Alice is seated round the table, with a drink, the atmosphere is low keyed out of respect, Conny appears and Alice makes the effort to make the gathering happier.

"Morning girls, hope your alright? Alice feeling a bit better?"

He kneels beside her.

"I thought that you the girls 'an me could take a trip down to see your mother the weekend: don't worry we'll wait in a pub somewhere' what'd think Alice? How a 'bout it girls?!

The response was over passionately overwhelming.

"Good idea Conny."

"Well that's settled that then, just before we go though, I thought we might slip in a little visit over Knightsbridge, look over the Army' n Navy store, got some nice schmutter 'n there, pay for trip 'n booze."

They all nod in agreement.

"You feel up to it Alice?"

"Yuh, count me in."

THURSDAY MORNING: THE FOURSOME ARRIVE AT KENSINGTON HIGH STREET.

They come in separate cabs keeping a distance between themselves, they let an interval of several minutes between entering the store and meeting at a pre=determined spot. Arrange to go into the ladies toilet, putting an 'out of order' notice on the door handle, to make doubly sure, one of the girls produce a small wooden wedge, to jam at the threshold of the door.

After deciding on their plan of action, they make their way to the agreed allotted rendezvous, it was to be their lucky day, although clothes were sparse owing to the war, the store had arranged several designers to display their latest fashions, the store was buzzing, Alice had to take the back seat again as the trio went to work. They had agreed before hand with Conny that they were to go with small luxurious items, dress, jewellery, gloves, silk, scarves the kind of accessories that the well to do lady would dress up for a night at the theatre or opera. Patsy and Alice teamed up, Lillian and Linda would enter the jewellery department from one end whilst Patsy and Alice would saunter through the other, they slowly walked up to the counter taking note of the opposition, Lillian inconspicuously held two fingers up to her nose Linda took note, getting the attention of one of the assistants whilst Lillian put her bag on the counter.

"Alice keep close to me, when I make my move keep on my outside as I go past Linda."

Linda had now got the attention of the second assistant who had placed a display box on top of the counter; Lillian for her part has put a necklace around her neck admiring her image.

"What do you think of it my dear, does it suit me?"

"Yes madam, very much."

"I wonder, if you have a ring to accompany it, something to set it off?"

The assistant turns, Lillian glances in the mirror from the tray she lifted a set of earrings moving other items to fill the gap, Linda for her part thanked the assistant, walks slowly towards Lillian's hands the earring to Linda,

"Quick Alice, follow me."

Alice keeps to the side of Patsy, Linda hands the jewellery to Patsy who continues to walk through the department with Alice in close proximity.

Once out of the salon, they sit down conversing.

They should be through in a couple of minutes."

Patsy turns to look Alice eye to eye.

"Alice, Conny told us he wants you to have a go today, nothing too big or awkward, do you feel up to it?"

Alice slowly nods her head.

"Good girl, the first times always the hardest, once you've done it, you'll get the buzz, it never leaves yuh, trust me."

True to her work, Lillian and Linda walk through smiling acknowledging Patsy, they pass Patsy gives it a couple of minutes, they meet up in the team rooms to discuss their next heist.

"What we can do Alice is to let you get the next heist I'll be ay your side, back you up now they've got a little what they call a bridsmaid boutique, French or something, anyway they got some nice little items, you know imitation jewellery, bits 'n pieces people buy the bride, not that I've had the chance…"

They both laugh.

Anyway I'll have the carpet bag on, ready to slip the items in, now all you gotta do is remember what us girls 'ave being doing up to yet, look the assistant in the eye, watch the body language, no sudden moves, keep her occupied in conversation, point out things behind her so that she has to turn her back on you for seconds, that's when you make your move, remember you got the upper 'and, she ain't suspecting anything from a young, cultured lady like you whose just come out of finishing school, above all be confident, talk slowly."

Patsy looks her in the eye.

"You alright Alice? You can do this."

Alice nods her head.

"Finish your tea, then we go."

The duo walks slowly out of the tea room casually glancing at the different items on display, picking odd items up, engaging in small talk.

On entering the boutique Patsy with a movement of her eyes , directs Alice to a counter displaying the small gifts and trinkets Patsy described earlier, Patsy lets Alice take the lead, going up to the counter full on, she notices a set of small silver spoons under the glass, then looking further along a box of serviette holders, looks to Patsy for approval, Patsy blinks her eyes, a gesture of 'yes'. The assistant comes over, Alice asks to look at the spoons, they are positioned on the counter.

"Is Madam going for a gift?"

Alice is lost for words, she tries to speak but no words come out, Patsy watching, as quick as a flash drops her small purse on the counter, the iron clasp makes a noise, it brings Alice back to her concentration and she feigns a cough.

"Er yes just a small token."

"Yes Madam but if you mind me saying so , the smaller gifts mean more sometimes."

Alice places the spoons in the blue silver box.

"Could I have a look at the serviette holders please?"

As the assistant turns Alice opens the box takes out the spoons, hands them to Patsy who is admiring some porcelain figurines, the assistant places the serviette holders on the counter, Alice picks them up, eyes them, leaves them on the counter.

"Could I have a look at those brandy glasses please?"

The assistant turns to get them from a display cabinet, she feels heavy breathing on her neck, a hand is placed on her wrist.

"Excuse me madam, we don't want any fuss but would you mind accompanying me to the manager office?"

Alice freezes, she looks desperately to Patsy for help – Patsy was quick to analyse the situation, turning round to look for her backups, she takes the large hat pin from her hate, jabs it as hard as she count into the top of the store detectives wrist, he lets out an ear-splitting yell, goes down on one knee to try to stem the flow of blood.

"Alice quick, follow me."

They both run out of the department, down to the fire escape doors, Lillian and Linda waiting a few strides away bring a mannequin into the path of the now pursing detective, he stops and tries to negotiate a way around them , each time he does they move to block his entrance.

"What on earths going on? Where's your manners young man?"

"I'm a store detective madam, I am trying to apprehend two felons now would you please let me through."

"That's no excuse to conduct your business, what's that blood on your hand coming through that handkerchief? Are you sure you're not running from the police or something?"

"No Madam, I can assure you I'm a bona fide store detective."

Slowly reluctantly, they walk away from the mannequin, which is now on the floor, he bends to pick it up, but the weight at the foot of it is too much, he loses his balance, as he only

Leverage of one hand, subsequently he falls headlong on top of the mannequin, Lillian and Linda walk slowly away, splitting up to mingle with the punters. For their part, Patsy and Alice walk quickly out of the ground level fire-exit to jump into a taxi.

An hour later the foursome are back at the "Eagle" drinking and laughing.

Conny walks in, sits down with them

"What's all the frivolity about girls?"

In between drinks, they all add to the story, finishing up with the escapade being the punch line. Conny laughs impressed at the girls ingenuity of quick thinking under pressure.

"So Alice, that's your first bit of excitement, whad'yuh think of it?"

Alice looks up starts to cry, then laughs. "Don't worry, it's the delayed reaction – nerves."

"It was alright."

"Wanna do it again?"

"Certainly."

"You know, I knew I wasn't wrong about you:- You've come a long way since pushing prams down the street."

Over the next two weeks Alice indulges in the one-off shoplifting. She becomes a deft hand, leading to Conny to becoming second in charge of a new group of girls.

Chapter 8

IN ALICE'S HOUSE: LATE AFTERNOON

Alice is relaxing in a chair holding up to the light a reproduction necklace, there is a knock on the door, bracing herself for the inevitable bad news on her mother, she hesitates at the door, waiting for the next knock, opening the door to reveal the young telegraph boy, he solemnly hands her the telegram, she slowly opens it, to read the message that her father had fallen at Pashendale, she reads it again, stares at the messenger.

"Will there be any reply Mum?"

She slowly nods her head no, slowly crushing the paper into her hand, closes the door, sits on the stairs sobbing quietly.

Later that night she visits Aunt Nora to tell her the news, they both sit down to have a drink/

"Are you going to tell the girls?"

"No, I think the little darling have been through enough already, are they alright, enjoying themselves I mean?"

"Yuh happy as pigs in a trough if you know what I mean, they money you give 'em to buy clothes, 'n food what more could they want, your right though, you can tell 'em later, don't wanna upset the little darlings."

AT HER MOTHERS BEDSIDE

Alice is in polite conversation with her mother's doctor –

"Yes I'm very sorry to hear about your father's death but I don't think it would be appropriate to break the news to her just yet, the shock could take away all the good work we've managed to headway with her."

"Oh alright you know best, but if I don't tell her, there won't be any way she could find out is there?"

"No, we don't allow newspapers to any of the patients, the only way the news might slip through the net is that if somebody might mention it in the hospital gossip."

"Thank you doctor if I could see her."

"That'll be alright but try not to get her too excited, or make her laugh, the act could bring on a coughing spell bring up blood."

Alice goes to her mother's ward, looks at one of two patients she is deeply shocked at the scene, then looks straight ahead, positioning her eye-line, blocking out groaning wheezing, coughing of the bed ridden patients, suddenly from nowhere, a patient walks up to her, she is in a daze, grabs at Alice's coat, Alice pulls back in shock – an orderly rushes up to gently take the patient away, Alice get her composure back before she reaches her mother's bed, gently kissed her on the head.

"Hello Mum."

Holding back the tears.

"How they treating you, getting enough to eat?"

Her mother's voice is very low, husky, rasping, Alice has to bend down to hear her.

"Yuh well enough, how's the girls? I wanna come home as soon as possible."

"Course you do mum, wait to get a little bit better – the girls are always asking about you , Nora's looking after them fine."

Her mother's eyes are filled with tears, she cannot cry openly as this would bring on a coughing fir again, Alice wipes her mother's eyes.

The meeting lasted another ten minutes until an orderly arrived to say it was time to leave.

"Mum I'm going to leave some money at the matrons office, if there's anything you want, just ask, there should be enough to see you over till my next visit."

They gently embrace, Alice leaves. In the visiting area, Alice has a word with the matron, handing her an envelope, she agrees to Alice's wishes. Outside, Alice find a corner to breakdown and cry. At the train station, she makes sure she finds an empty compartment, contemplating on the way home how her life has to pan out.

A MONTH LATER

Alice, Conny are now an item, They are walking through Hyde park their feeling for one another were plain to see, stopping to buy an ice cream, they sit down on a park bench by the Serpentine.

!I was thinking Conny, how long can we keep this caper up? I mean we've nearly had our collars felt a couple of times, an' I'm running out of all the different colours of wigs."

They both laugh.

"Well, as I see it business is good, we've recruited some intelligent girls, which obviously means when they go holstering they ain't easily recognizable and the ol' bill leave us alone, we pay em' off, there's no violence, mind you, put some money away for a nest egg, y'never know girl."

Alice doesn't reply, just gazing at the Serpentines atmosphere, contemplating.

HER HOUSE THAT NIGHT

Alice and Conny are drinking a knock on the door.

"Want me to get it luv?"

"No don't worry."

Alice opens the door to be confronted by the Doctor, she feels the colour draining from her face - she knew straight away the significance of the doctors appearance, she holds back her emotions.

"I'm so sorry Alice."

"Did she die with no pain, that's the most important thing Doctor."

"Yes Alice, she dies in her sleep at four o'clock, we have no cure for T.B. as yet, all they could do was to administer the drugs to ease the pain, you've been a good daughter to her Alice, she had the best care she could have."

"Thank you Doctor, I'll come round tomorrow to organize the funeral arrangements."

Alice's walks back into the embracing arms of Conny, sobbing uncontrollably.

"That's right 'ol girl, let it all come out."

NEXT DAY: LATE MORNING

Alice arrives at Nora's house, hesitates before she knocks, the door opens, straight away Nora knew the mind-set they both hug one another, in the background she could hear the girls laughing, enjoying themselves.

"She died peacefully Nora, - how are the girls?"

"They've been no trouble at all eating well, always well-dressed with the money you give me to clothe 'em, well-mannered what else could you ask for?"

They walk into the parlour.

"How am I going to explain to them, it would spoil their little world?"

"Best to get it over with quick, I'll call 'em."

The girls rush in to put their arms around Alice who bends down to greet them.

"Have you been good girls for Aunt Nora?"

"Of course Alice."

Both in unison.

"How's mummy?"

"Come 'n sit down with me, one on each knee."

The girls are excited.

"Girls, mummy's no longer with us, she's gone to live with the angels, but before she went she told me that she loved you more than anything in the whole world."

"More than we love you Alice?"

"Much, much more."

The girls start to cry, hugging Alice tighter, she cries.

"You're not going to the angels are you Alice?"

"No of course not, I'll be with you all the time."

The girls clung tight to Alice, not speaking, their vulnerability was easy to understand, Nora watched the scene unravel unto after fifteen minutes she gently took them into the backroom where they sat quietly together, she stayed with them for several minutes, then went back to Alice.

"Nora I want to ask you a big favour, would it be possible for the girls to stay with you after the funeral, I've gotten involved with some people which allows me to earn some proper money to help bring up the kids, I can delay telling 'em about dad, can you help me?"

"Don't worry about it Alice love, It'll be alright for a while, the only thing is, I don't want to know what kind of business you've gotten involved in, so long as you promise me nobody gets hurt?"

"They won't Nora, thanks very much."

Nora gets out a bottle of gin with two glasses, they indulge for a period of time, reminiscing old memories.

TWO WEEKS LATER: DAY CHURCH GRAVEYARD

Alice with the two girls are by the open grave, crying the entourage surround the grave include Nora, Conny who is surrounded by all of the girls from the "Eagle".

Alice is in deep conversation with Conny.

"Well Alice I don't want to sound too pushy, but have you decided which way you wanna go: sorry what I mean is now you've got the children to look after, do you wanna call it a day, so you can care for them full time, or do you wanna still work with the girls?"

"Conny I've got to be honest, It wasn't hard to come to a decision, if I don't work for you, with the washing business finished, there won't be any money coming in to the house, no money, no rent, we'll be on the streets but Nora's willing to look after the girls but I gotta pay, clothe 'em, feed 'em – I'll still see 'em regularly, it's a no brainer, I still wanna work with yuh, if you'll have me?"

Conny embraces her

"That's what I wanted to hear Alice, give it a bit of time, let things settle down, it'll turn out alright, you'll see."

THREE MONTHS LATER

Alice had moved up the hierarchy to be Conny's number 1, the other girls had no problem with this, Alice was a natural born leader, her confidence, quick thinking didn't go unnoticed around South London criminal fraternity. She had become more aggressive, but had a split personality when she was in the company of Nora, her two sisters. They were always well dressed, well behaved and people used to give the trip a second look when they were walking or in a good class of restaurant in South London, things were going well for them, until one fatal incident upset the doctored atmosphere.

Alice, with five of her gang were having a quiet drink on the borders of her manor, they kept a low profile as it was recognized that the different elements didn't venture on one another's territory.

In a corner of the pub, three men getting more inebriated by the minute started to zone in on the girls slowly sauntering over to ask the girls if they wanted a drink, Alice taking the lead, politely said no, the men felt insulted, asking if their money wasn't good enough, one started to put his arm around one of the girls, she looks to Alice for guidance, now feeling intimidated, Alice nods her head she jumps up, leans across the table and from the sleeve of her coat she produces a "black jack", swipes it across the assailants head, he falls to the floor, knocked out the other girls jump up, taking the hat pins from their hats and go to stab the men's faces and hands, they scream in pain, the girls follow this up by smashing bottles across their head, leaving the fallen victims on the floor they beat a hasty retreat to the toilets. The girls started to laugh, compose themselves look to Alice, she nods her head to the door.

The incident did not go unnoticed by two middle aged men sitting at the bar, as the girls disappeared into the outside.

A DAY LATER. ALICE'S HOUSE

Alice and Conny are in bed together, Alice had just finished telling him about the escapade at the pub Conny does not respond straight away, Alice is a bit perturbed by the silence.

"What's the matter Conny, have I said something wrong?"

Conny sits up in bed, lights a cigarette, takes a long draw before answering, looking straight ahead.

"That little escapade you got involved with the other day happened to be some gang members from Islington, they didn't take to it very kindly, they will probably want to pay is a visit…"

"Hang on a minute Conny, they started it, we had to protect ourselves, you would've done the same…"

"That ain't the point Alice, they lose face, especially as a bunch of girls turned 'em over."

"Well it happened now, what can we do about it?"

"Nothing much, just keep a low profile, see how it unfolds."

He gets dressed leaves, Alice is left pondering on the event, what might become.

THREE DAYS LATER DAY: THE "CUT" WATERLOO

Conny, with two of his gang are drinking at a coffee stall, suddenly two cars silently appear from each end of the road – five men jump out of each, tear into Conny, his two friends are beaten to the ground – in the Melee Conny is savagely beaten his head hitting the curb, loses consciousness to make matters worse the protagonists pour cups of coffee over them, and drive off.

Alice is in the "Eagle" when the news is broken to her and the girls, they all get cabs between them and go to St. Thomas' Hospital, entering Conny's room, she stops dead in her tracks, he is bandaged head to foot, one leg is suspended in a swing, both his arms spread across his chest. His head is heavily bandaged, only for his eyes and moth to be visible, he slowly tries to raise his arm, gives up. Alice slowly walks over to sit by his bed side she kisses him gently a nurse comes in.

"You can stay with him for five minutes."

Alice nods, she cannot speak to him, just lays her head on the pillow beside his head.

A DAY LATER "THE EAGLE"

Alice, all the girls are seated around their reserved table, the mood is sombre, Conny's minders are just finishing their drinks.

"Well girls it looks like we got a pretty serious problem on our hands, those geezers from Islington have made their move, they're waiting to see what reaction were gonna come up with as far as I can see it, we've got a couple of options, we can let it go, in which case they might see it as a victory leaving it open for them to muscle in on our territory…"

He looks around to the group, he has their full attention.

"The other option is to enlist the help of the East London boys, they've helped us out before – they owe us a couple of favours."

Alice interrupts. "Yuh that's alright in the short turn, but would we have to give up some of our control from the old bill for the protection rackets, the fences who keep us in business?"

"Fair point Alice, but we gotta find a solution pretty sharpish, they'll make their move soon enough and we gotta be ready."

Linda speaks up.

"What about if we have a parley with 'em, maybe iron out the problem before it goes too far, we've got nothing to lose either way?"

The girls murmur their approval.

"It ain't as easy as that Linda, they'll want their cut of the action, no losing face, list, me and the boys'll have a little parley later, see what we can come up with, right lets 'ave a drink."

HOSPITAL LATER THAT NIGHT

Alice is sitting by the side of Conny's bed, whispering in his ear, he moves two of his unbandaged fingers, she smiles, kisses him on the lips, leaves.

A DAY LATER. A PUB IN EAST LONDON

Conny's second in command Jack, with two members of the gang are seated around a table also occupied with three members of the "Titanic Gang" the conversation was low keyed owing to the fact they didn't want to be over heard.

"What we have here is a problem concerning your little fracas with the North London boys I'll come straight to the point, 1. You can carry on the vendetta, which would lead to more aggro or 2. You could offer them some sort of recompense that way nobody loses face, if not this business is gonna get silly, everybody loses."

 "What'd mean, what we gotta to offer?"

"What they would like is part of your action, you take on some of their girls in your shop hoistering, learn em the ropes until they got the hang of things, then call it a day, it seems to me to make a bit of sense, we don't want the status quo changed, the ole' bill start taking an interest in the commotion, everybody's on edge, what'd you think?"

Jack ponders on the proposition, he looks to Alice, she nods in approval, Jack pauses.

"Okay, we'll make arrangements."

"Good, it seems a sensible outcome under the circumstances – by the way Alice, that geezer you used that 'Black Jack' on, 'es got a right bump on his hooter, he ain't too pleased about it, you can handle yourself alright…"

"I did tell him no, he wouldn't take it for an answer."

"I totally agree, still I wouldn't like to meet you on a dark night."

They laugh.

TWO DAYS LATER. DAY HOSPITAL

Alice is waiting in the reception area a doctor walks over to her sits down, Alice senses something is wrong by his body language.

"Alice, you don't mind if I call you Alice?"

"There's been some complication set in since I saw you last, Conny has bloody poisoning, we've tried all the drugs we have at hand but the infection has taken hold and is spreading all over his body, the next twelve hours will be very critical one way or the other…"

"He's a strong person, but with blood poisoning it can quickly turn to gangrene in all of his limbs, I don't have to describe to you if we have to amputate what he would end up like".

Alice nods, holds back her tears, emotions.

"Thank you for being so honest and candid doctor, I know he wouldn't be able to take the amputation I'll come by tomorrow Doctor."

"I'm sorry that I couldn't be more positive."

On her way out, Alice finds an empty linen room, lets herself in, breaks down to sob uncontrollably.

NEXT DAY. THE INJURED GANGSTERS FLOP HOUSE

A group of men are seated around a table drinking and smoking. The main man lays a flush on the table.

"The way I see it is we ain't got nothing to lose, a couple of you get a spanking, I can live with that, if you can."

He scans the group to see the reaction.

"Right that's settled then, the main thing is we get inroad to their little scam, once we get the full S.P we can leave whenever we want, no love lost, it ain't no L.S.D so we go ahead with it."

"All agreed? Good. Kenny, you set up a meeting to iron out the finer details."

That afternoon Alice is walking down the corridor to Conny's room. She goes to enter, but the doctor bars her way.

"Alice come to my office."

Alice duly follows, they sit down opposite one another.

"Alice, we couldn't stop the poisoning, he had a heart attack then a stroke, He died peacefully and hour ago."

Alice is mortified, she stares at a picture on the wall she feels herself coming over faint, tries to support herself, the doctor rushes forward to support her before she hits the floor, he helps her to an examination couch, gently lays her out.

TEN MINUTES LATER

Alice slowly comes round, tries to get up from beside the couch, a nurse aids her.

"Don't get up too quick Miss, you might fall over."

Alice nods slowly slumps back to the couch, the doctor enters.

"How you feeling Alice, can we get in touch with somebody to take you home?"

"That would be helpful Doctor, I'll contact one of my friends."

A while later, Alice is in the reception area, when the two girls walk in, they wait for Alice to speak.

"Well girls, were on our own now, we'll have to have a little parley round the 'Eagle' tomorrow to sour out our strategy for the future."

The girls hold Alice's arms as they walk out to a waiting taxi, as they help her in they both look at one another, seemingly not understanding the coldness of her presence, with no remorse.

THE EAGLE NEXT MORNING

Alice, the gang are sitting around a table in the back room, noticeably Alice has taken the position in Conny's chair at the head of the table, and they are all silent until Alice looks around at each of those present.

"Well girls let's get down to business, Conny'll be buried next week, I hope there will be a big turnout, he'd like that…"

All the gang nod, tapping the table.

"After the burial I'm going to meet the leader of that 'Titanic' gang see If we can iron out some of our differences before they get out of hand, when that's done we'll get back into business. Agreed? Right let's get rid of this sombre mood, the drinks are on me. Oh by the way, I'd like all of you to get a 'black jack', practice how to use it, it could get you out of trouble in the future, which you can be rest assured is going to come."

THE WEEK LEADING UP TO CHRISTMAS: INSIDE THE EAGLE

The gang had a good week, the atmosphere was as one would expect, the girls were in a boisterous mood, over the intermediate months they had got more confident, more aggressive, taken on more ambitious projects, this led to more jealousy from different gangs because the 'forty thieves' had the backing of the local gang. From out of nowhere, the atmosphere changed, voices were raised, bottles started to crash and splints on the already wet beer floor then the high pitch battle between two opposing groups of women. In a few minutes the male factions had to take one side or the other, then it became a free for all brawl. After ten minutes bystanders pulled the main perpetrators apart, a group left the pub, the remaining locals quietened down for a while, but not before they got even more intoxicated, they still had the urge for another fight.

Half an hour later a large group made their way round to whom they believed started the fight, Alice was that the forefront, banging on the door, when it opened a jug full of water was thrown over her, incensed, she ordered her gang to smash down the door armed with knives, iron bars, black jacks, they wreaked havoc in the house, lashing out at anybody who got in their way, more followed from the 'Eagle', those who couldn't get in the pub started to throw bricks , bottles, anything else that was at hand at the windows of the building. The fracas went on for half an hour until the advance of police whistles announced they had to scarper in the melee, Alice was in the parlour of the house, owing to the intruders pushing their way in, she couldn't escape.

She was arrested, hand cuffed with her trusted lieutenants, led away to a waiting Black Maria, to spend the night in the cells to be charged the next day, the to the local magistrates court.

Alice received a twelve month sentence that she served in the Holloway prison, inside she was a model prisoner to be rewarded by getting special privileges by the screws. Owing to the fact that when she was allowed visitors the screws were well rewarded by the girls, luxuries, the prison wardens could only dream of.

Alice was kept up to date with the state of affairs, mainly wanting to know if any particular women or group was about to take over her hierarchy. The girls assured her there was no problem there, everything would return to normal as soon as she was release. The shoplifting was cut back, but this served a good purpose, it gives the stores a false picture. They would carry on as normal, taking the stores by surprise. Alice once again showing her leadership, thinking, beyond the prison walls.

TEN MONTHS LATER – HOLLOWAY PRISON GATES

Owing to her good behaviour Alice got two months remission. A large car pulls up, Alice who has all her belongings in a black bag, chucks it up into the air, just before getting into the back of the car, the contents spewing across the road, the light objects blow away in the wind, passing people look on in amazement.

"Where to Alice?" Linda asks.

"I think a little pub I know called the 'Eagle' I hear you can get a nice quiet drink there with no trouble. The clientele are supposed to be the best hosts this side of South London."

The girls all cheer, Alice is handed a tumbler.

"What's this? I've changed my ways, I don't partake in any kind of dubious drinking habits, I'm a reformed lady, just you watch."

Without further ado, she emptied the half-filled tumbler without a breather.

The girls lapped this up, a bottle was passed round to top up all the empty glasses.

On arrival at the 'Eagle' the door was closed there wasn't a soul in sight. Alice looked forlornly at the door.

"Bleeding 'ell, what's going on here you ain't decided to hold a wake here, just on my sodding release?"

The girls say nothing, bowing their heads, they slowly shuffle towards the door, one of them knocks, no reply, she tries the handle looks around shakes her head dismissively opens her hands, at that instant the doors burst open, a jazz band starts playing 'for she's a jolly good women'

Alice holds back her tears as she slowly walks through a semi-guard of honour into the saloon bar which is decked out with a large decoration of bunting, a table in the middle of the room takes prominence with a large cake modelled on a store with the names of Selfridges, Derry&Tom, Army & Navy Store, Whiteleys.

Alice is handed a full tumbler of spirits and a large cake knife to cut the cake, this got the full approval of the entourage.

"Speech, Speech!"

Alice smiles, clears her throat.

"Unaccustomed as I am to this kind of gathering, as you know I'm a shy home loving girl…"

Her speech is drowned out by whistles, laughter.

"I would just like to thank you all for the wonderful reception, and keeping faith in me, and the operations were involved with; without further ado, I declare this home coming part to commence in full swing, bless you all. By the way, we start tomorrow, just to get hand in again."

She raises her hand to crack her knuckles, the crowd lap it up, and the band starts playing again.

Alice catches the eye of Conny's right hand fixer, he saunters over, they embrace.

"Nice to have you back again Alice, we all missed you."

"Well I certainly missed you lot, how's business been?"

"Well we kept to what you said, we started on the outer town stores, we hoisted a good little pot, the ole' bill left us alone, we done alright on the summer sales up West, we now eating for the Christmas sales, I reckon they think we've gone away, so their security could be a little lapse."

"I wouldn't bank on that Jack, they ain't silly, they know by now I'm out, so there gonna start tightening up their security, we'll have a little parley tomorrow, go over a few things, decide what our strategy gonna be - by the way 'ows the 'Islington Boys' treating yuh, everything alright?"

"Well Alice that's what I want to have a little word with you in private."

The party went on till the early hours of the morning.

From across the road, in the shadows, three men were taking down notes of who was coming, and who was going from the 'Eagle'.

Alice and Jack were sitting in the parlour drinking.

"Well Alice, it's really nice to have you back nothing changed much, we tightened up our operation, only recruited a couple of new girls, there coming on a bundle, you can meet 'em in the week, see what you think of 'em, we've straightened out our problems with the gangs, sorted out our territories 'an everything."

"We've got a new snout in the old bill, he's been good to us, don't wanna lose 'im…"

"Well Jack, what can I say, if your happy, I'm happy, while I was catered for at his majesty's pleasure I had plenty of time to think, gotta a couple of ideas, I wanna put to the test, this snout you got, I'd like to meet him, is that possible?"

"Yuh I can arrange that, take a couple of days to up mind you."

"That's fine, let's have another tiddly wink, take the taste of the 'Doctor Crippen' away."

They both laugh.

Chapter 9

TWO DAYS LATER, ALICE AND THE SNOUT ARE IN A NICKELODEON ARCADE

The two are in the shadows, both looking in opposite directions.

"All I want to know is when the next women's suffrage movement is taking place in the West End, mainly Oxford Street, roughly the number of police taking control, the time, where it starts 'n finishes."

"That shouldn't be too hard, that kind of info' easy to come by, the force is well rehearsed, we've got our snouts in the movement."

"Good now you get that information as soon as and I'll meet you in the 'Trocadero' two days' time."

"By the bar, I'll start to dance when the 'excuse me' waltz start, you break in, have what I asked you for on a piece of paper put it in my hand, walk away when the dance finishes."

"Blimey Alice, all what I've heard about you, I'll take back, I didn't know they took dancing lessons in Holloway, or was it at your finishing school?"

They both laugh, leave in opposite directions.

TWO DAYS LATER: MID AFTERNOON. THE ROCADERO

The band is in full swing, Alice is dancing with one of the professional dancers, it ends, Alice looks round still holding her partner, the M.C makes his announcement.

"Ladies and Gentleman the next two dances will be a waltz, there will be two numbers, the first one will be an 'excuse me', will the gentlemen kindly note that when they are tapped on the shoulder you should immediately give up your partner, thank you."

The music started, Alice falls into step with her partner, she forcibly smiles, engaging in small talk, her eyes looking round her new partner, her dancing partner is getting a bit agitated at Alice's uninteresting answers to his question.

"Excuse me."

Alice smiles, breathes a sigh of relief, the snout had arrived, placing his hand in hers, he lets go of a piece of paper, Alice quickly puts it in her small dress bag, after several minutes there was another "excuse me", Alice settles down, but keeps looking at the clock, forcefully smiling until the torturous waltz had finished.

Getting a cab home, she looked at the information, using a pen to gauge a distance between the dates, satisfied, smiles all the way home, her plan had already begun to take shape in her head.

POLICE STATION: WEST END CENTRAL

A group of policeman, uniformed, plain clothes are seated around a table. The leader takes the platform.

"Ok everybody, can I have your attention, in three days time the 'suffragettes' are planning a demonstration from Oxford Circus, up to Marble Arch, then down Park Lane, then back to Speakers Corner in Hyde Park. The Prime Minister is not very happy with the situation, to say the least, if he bring the army out it won't look any good if it gets out of hand, which it will, he's afraid that the 'agent provocateurs will infiltrate the march and turn it into a political fracas, unfortunately we're caught up in the little maelstrom, ;an I don't have to tell you lot we'll get the blame whichever way it goes, picking up the pieces, also I'll have to answer for the overtime bill..."

Sniggers, he looks round, the perpetrators lower their heads.

"I've had order from up above that we are to keep a low profile as possible, if you have to physically man-handle any of the marchers, try to use as much finesse as you can, within reason, nit at the same time protect yourselves, that's all. On your way out the clerk will give all the information of times, positioning of the police members etc, when you've explained it all to your squads, destroy the paper, I don't want it to get into the wrong hands."

Alice's snout slowly waits his turn to take the information sheet. That afternoon Alice is at the local library, choosing a book at random she sits down at a table, several minutes later, the snout sits at the other end, flipping through the pages of his book he slides and envelope between the covers, several minutes later he walks past Alice putting the book on an adjacent chair, Alice puts her bag over it, slipping her hand beneath the bag, she retrieves the envelope, [;acing it inside her shawl, wait for a few minutes then leaves.

TWO HOURS LATER: ALICE'S HOUSE

Alice is sitting alone at a table, spread out in front of her is a large piece of white paper, off the paper is the information sheet that the police informer was given, she draws two parallel lines across the paper with a cross road in the middle, labels it Oxford Circus then Regent Street, naming three stores, which she designates with the match boxes she keeps glancing at the notes, jotting down times, police numbers, then fills in the blank road with a red pen, then over lays with the word 'Disturbance', sitting back slowly drinking a spirit, contemplates the pros and cons of her method of attack, getaway, number of how many of the girls she will use.

TWO HOURS LATER

She has several large sheets overlapping the original sheet, seemingly satisfied with her conclusion , gazes into mid-air, folds up the complete package, pulls back a large rug in front of the fire grate then uses a small coal shovel to life up a loose floor board, moves her 'Black Jack' to make room for her paperwork.

THE 'EAGLE' NEXT DAY. BACK ROOM.

Alice with all of her gang are seated at the table, Jack who has taken the place of Conny, has two if his gang sitting each side of him.

"Well Alice, hope the ol' brains ticking over, the boys are getting itchy feet."

"Not to worry, I've worked something out, needs a bit of refining but I think the overall plan should work…"

From beside her chair, she opens a carpet-bag lays the sheet of paper on the table, they all go quiet.

"Right, number one, all what I'm going to explain will have to be kept in your heads, there won't be any written instruction, this is to safeguard my source."

The next hour is spent explaining her plan.

"Now it's just like all the other heist's we've done, but this time, we've got the added advantage of the demonstration doing all the ground work for us, the police contingent will be stretch to the limit, any added disturbances they'll put down to part of demonstration, they've been told not to move from any of their allotted positions, making our job getting in, the getaway will just look like another incident, any questions?"

"Supposing I wanna join the demonstration, I'm all for law 'n order."

It broke the concentration, they all laugh.

"We'll meet up in two days' time, remember no loose talk keep schtum, now let's have a drink."

TWO DAYS LATER. THE 'EAGLE'

Alice, the girl gang, six of the male gang are mingling.

"Right, everybody, you know all of your instructions, remember, keep it tight if you have to use any persuading measures, use 'em."

"We cannot allow the ol' bill to organize themselves, there'll be in numbers, we got surprise on our side, just use it, ok let's get on with it."

The atmosphere was tense, they all knew this was to be different from any of their other forays, they went out in groups of three at several minutes intervals, as not to make the emptying of the pub suspicious.

The cars were parked at different locations, some around the corner and others down alley-ways, the last one adjacent outside a parade of shops.

The journey to the West End was uneventful until they got to the bottom of Tottenham Court Road, the police were diverting the traffic away, this did not deter the gangs route, when they were stopped, they showed their fake press passes what the police snout had supplied, waving them through they went through the side streets running parallel to Oxford Street, where they pulled up, staggering the distances between the cars. As they got out they could hear the noise of the demonstration in the near vicinity; walking into the demonstration they kept tightly knitted, using their large carpet bags to force their way through the throngs.

Getting near the front windows of the stores the police formed a human chain, intermingled with mounted police, the atmosphere was starting to get unruly, the professional agitators started to take over the semi-disciplined atmosphere of the demonstration, high pitched in to apprehend whistles echoed around the milling crows. The police pitched in to apprehend the ring leaders, the horses rearing up led their handlers to wade in the melee, pandemonium now broke out, bricks, fire-crackers, anything that came to hand was used against the police, the office stewards, peacemakers, could do nothing to quell the out of control crowd , this was the chance Alice was waiting for, she signalled to the gang who were in touching distance of one another to make their way to the entrance of the store, demonstrators before them had took refuse in the space, the doors were forced open, the agitators took this as their opportunity to storm into the store, the once peacefully demonstration turned into a 'free for all', the police lost control of the situation, Alice, the girls rant to their allotted positions, filling up their bags with the most expensive items they could muster, the male members of the gang making they were not molested by the police, or store detectives, once they had filled their carpet bags, the pockets in their coats, each group was led to a back stairway to the awaiting cars, getting into the cars caused a small problem, the boots had to be opened to put the bags in the back, this down, they slowly made their way back through the deserted back streets taking a different route back to their rendezvous point, the 'Eagle'.

'EAGLE' NIGHT

The cars came at fifteen minute intervals the girls, men carrying the spoils through to the back of the pub, they were all excited but held their feelings to themselves, until they were in the closed confines of the back room, where they positioned all the goods out on to a long table. After the last group came in they bolted both doors, Alice started to pick through the collection her smile getting larger until she had finished her inspection.

"Girls, you surpassed my high hopes, your choice of hoisting is one of the best yet, you can all be assured you'll get a good bonus for this lot..."

The girls cheered, Alice moves her hands to hush them up.

"By the time the owners make their inventory of the damage, losses of goods, they'll blame it on the demonstrators rampaging through the store, that takes a lot of pressure off is for the time being, ok, if we can spend a couple of hours bagging this lot up, I can appraise everything before we take to the fences, right let's get on with it have a little top of drinks just to keep your minds on the job."

Alice takes Jack to one side.

"Jack you sure none of the old bill noticed out girls working in groups, because if they did we might get a visit from 'em?"

"No, don't worry Alice, there was so much pandemonium going on, it was everybody for themselves, the ol' bill didn't know which way to look, y'know what, we could do with more of those demonstrations, it'll make our job more easy."

"Chance would be a fine thing."

SUMMER 1925

For Alice things were on the up and up, she had accrued herself a small fortune which was privately banked plus she had the added insurance of diamond rings that adorned each finger on every hand. The 'Forty Elephants' has become more organized with Alice's direction, guaranteed with the added protection of the 'Elephant Boys' certain police officers came under an umbrella who afforded them protection, giving members of the gang who were arrested, the opportunity to a bribe, or getting a lighter sentence.. Alice was not a greedy gang leader ordering her girls not to be greedy, this in turn was rewarded by a grudging respect by the police.

On one of her walks through London dong a recognisance for another job, she came across an orphanage. Walking past the wall she came to an iron gate that when she got up close she see the children playing in the playground, she was taken aback, mesmerized she was there for several minutes until a shadow behind fell across the gate.

"Can I help you Madam?"

She quickly turns around, a policeman is staring at her, instantly recognizes her.

"Sorry Alice, I thought you might be one of those funny people, we've had some reports of perverts looking at the kids."

"That's alright officer, what is this place?"

"Its Dr Barnado's orphanage, he takes the ragged children off the street, looks after them, teaches them a trade if can, better than living off the streets, doing a good job I reckon!"

"Your right, thank you officer."

"Take care Alice."

TWO DAYS LATER

Alice is in an office sitting opposite the head administrator of the orphanage. It is a well conducted meeting.

"Well Miss Diamond I fully appreciated your interest in giving one of our pupils a home, but I must emphasise that we have to have a deep and through history of the child's would be new parents, the criteria which we most endorse is that the child is well looked after, not being traumatised from their original situation, you understand? This brings me onto your personal position, marriage status etc, we would have to inspect your house to see that the child is brought up in the right environment, is there anything you wish to ask me?"

"Well if I could take it point by point, I am single at the moment, but engaged to my fiancé, to be married in the very near future, I live in a very nice comfortable house, which is very cosy, homely, the area has all facilities a child would like, all the amenities local parks, a library, but most of all good schools, and a welcoming safe home."

"Well we don't work on a point system, but what age, male, female a local child. Someone from the country those kind of thing, you have to take into consideration, interestingly enough we do have a three year old child who we have just taken in, a tragic case – her parents were killed in a house fire, the neighbours fire brigade were left helpless, the child was dropped out of the window into the arms of a policeman, the parents were overcome with smoke."

Alice is quietly overcome, gets out her handkerchief to wipe away a tear, the administrator picks up the body language.

"Yes a truly tragic case, never the less we're doing our best to comfort her, well what I'd like to suggest is you go home, think very seriously about our conversation, what your taken on, come back to see us is a couple of days, after you've thought things over."

As Alice is being escorted the corridor of the school the administrator beckons Alice to look through the glass panelled door of one of the class rooms.

"You see how many children we take in, most of them are manageable, but we do have some who have withdrawal symptoms they're the ones who need all the love and affection."

At the school entrance, Alice shakes hand with the administrator, leaves, further down the road she starts to sob.

A week later Alice receives a letter asking her to attend the orphanage, she is shown into a large room, around the table are seated two women, a man who is introduced as a doctor, and the administrator who formally spoke to her a week he spoke first.

"Well Miss Diamond we have considered your application for adoption, the little girl is settling in well and we would not want to be disposed of upsetting the status quo you understand, I would go as far to sat if Rose is not adopted in the future, I believe that in our walls she will grow up, happy and stabilised, which we strive to achieve/ I would like to introduce you to our resident house keeper Miss McCarthy."

"Good morning Miss Diamond, obviously I notice you are not married, is there any reason for this?"

Alice was not expecting this question, and had to think quick for a satisfactory answer.

"Yes Miss McCarthy, I was engaged to my fiancé but he was tragically gassed in the trenches at Flanders, it did upset me greatly as we planned to start a family as soon as the war ended, when he was patriated."

The group pause, all making notes in their folders.

"I'm sorry to hear that Miss Diamond."

"Lady Simmons would like to speak to you now."

"Welcome Miss Diamond, from your letter of introduction, I take note that your profession comes under the heading of reclaimed clothes administrator. Could you expand on this please?"

"Basically, I purchase clothes off dealers who purchase the garments from stores when they have their end of season sales, or when fashion dictates that some of the garments are out of date, or slightly damaged. They are brought up to a respectable appearance, then I sell them for a small profit to the not so well of people in South London, also for the widowers of the war, we hold local charity events where they are auctioned off for a few pence."

"Admirable Miss Diamond, admirable no if you were to be successful in your application at this stage, we would have to inspect your lodgings for obvious reasons, where the child would sleep, safety measures, a happy environment, a local church, play area amenities, all the points that would encourage Rose to grow in a protected environment into a well-balance child to be a small pillar in the establishment."

"Yes Lady Simmons I believe that I could adhere to all the criteria that you've mentioned, obviously you would be more than welcome to visit my home and surroundings to allay any fears you have for Rose's environment."

Lady Simmons gazes at Alice in the eye for several seconds, her face is motionless, and then slowly breaks into a smile, once again they all take note in their files.

"I would like to introduce you to Doctor Barnaby, he is the resident doctor and health worker, he would liaise with you if your request is granted, visiting you at undisclosed times to make sure the child is being well looked after and safe: Dr Barnaby."

"Good morning Miss Diamond, I would like firstly to ask you if you are in good health, please be honest with me, as I have to check up your personal doctor, at the moment let us assume that don't have TB, whooping cough, measles, chicken pox that kind of thing, if we can clear that up now it would be very helpful and speed up the process enormously."

"No doctor, I could myself lucky that I don't have any of the complaints your mention, I could myself lucky on that aspect."

"Very good, do you foresee yourself getting married in the foreseeable future? I ask this question in the hope that the child will have a secure home?"

"I must admit Doctor that after my fiancé demise it will take a period of time to go down that road."

"Very good Miss Diamond, did you have a happy childhood? What I mean by that is did you live in a happy environment, your parents made you feel secure, do you have a happy outlook in life, forgive me for asking these personal questions but we do have to think of the child all the time, what kind of pressure she would come under, not to be physically abused, to grow up and to be respected in the community."

Alice pauses.

"I'll be perfectly honest with you doctor, I cannot answer yes to all your points because some are far reaching into the future, but for the earlier months, years hopefully, I would and will endeavour to carry out very positively, honestly with always keeping the child's health and future paramount, that's my behest."

The group all exchange glances, jotting down in their folders.

"Miss Diamond we will adjourn for the moment, the matron will bring you in some refreshments."

The group get up to leave to an adjoining room Alice consoles herself into gazing around the room, now that she is all alone, the noise of the children playing in the playground filter through the open windows, she smiles to herself drifting into a happy place she is brought back from her seclusion by the return of the group they sit down in silence, opening their folders, the head administrator looks up to Alice smiling.

"After carefully going through your answers to our questions, we are happy to announce that we believe you have the criteria and hopefully would make an ideal candidate for adoption, that is to say we will still have to make some final background checks, mainly visiting your home, the environment etc, once that has been completed and everything is acceptable to all of us, we can arrange the first meeting of the child to ascertain if the feelings are mutual,

I'm afraid at the conjecture we cannot give a definite yes or no, I hope you find this acceptable."

"Thank you so much, I appreciate your time and honesty, regarding your visit to my home it can be arranged at your earliest convenience."

"Would it be possible to see Rose now , without any contact obviously, before I leave?"

The group look at one another, they all nod their head positively.

"That's quite acceptable Miss Diamond, Miss McCarthy will escort you to the nursery, you'll be able to see the child through the door window. Well that concludes our meeting Miss Diamond, I'll write to you as soon as possible to arrange the meeting, thank you for your time, goodbye."

The group nods their head in acknowledgement, the matron walks over to Alice.

"If you would like to follow me Miss Diamond."

Alice didn't need any further prompting, she quickly followed behind to house keeper, bumps into her, apologizes, they go down a corridor to stop at two large doors with half windows, the house keeper beckons Alice to look through, she pushes her face up to the window, looking round until she zones in on Rose, who is playing with some dolls, Alice feels herself about to cry getting gout her handkerchief up to her face, she smiles, mesmerised, putting her hand on the window.

"Are you alright Miss Diamond? We have to go now it's time for their sleep."

"Thank you."

Outside the orphanage Alice walks along the road quietly sobbing to herself.

INSIDE ALICES HOUSE MORNING – THREE DAYS LATER.

Peering through her curtains she waits for the post man is just about to put a letter through the post box opens the door, takes the letter from his outstretched hand, he gives her a quizzical look.

"Be careful Alice, it could be a bill."

She looks at the post mark.

"No its definitely not a bill, thank you."

Closing the door she rushes into the parlour, slowly opens the letter, scans the wording.

"Dear Miss Diamond,

Further to out meeting Monday last I am glad to inform you that your application for adopting the child Rose has been gladly accepted fully by the panel. Could you please contact us at your earliest convenience to formalise all particulars.

Yours Sincerely,

M, Steward, Head Administrator."

Alice reads the letter twice, then starts to cry getting dressed she goes round to the 'Eagle' she goes to the back room where the ensemble of girls are having an early morning tete a tete

"Right girls down to business, I'm going to hire out the small mission hall down by the Broadway I want you to bring all your dresses, coats, any other clothes you can muster, I'd like to have it up and running by tomorrow morning, the people who will be visiting you are highly educated, pinnacle of society…"

"Just like us Alice."

Laughter.

"Be serious please ladies, you can guarantee you'll be asked personal questions!"

"Not too personal, we'd get arrested." There's laughter.

"Please, hear me out, just answer politely no bad language."

"What's this all about Alice, you going for membership of the women's institute?"

"I am going up for adoption of a child, now it all depends on the reaction that you girls give when they scrutinize your answers, just be pleasant, charming no slang talk, no trooper language, the whole decision relies on your girls."

All the girls look at one another, then break into a clapping whistling frenzy then a rendition of 'she's a jolly good fellow' they all take turns to hug her.

"Thank you girls, I know I could rely on you."

"Well this causes for a celebration, open the bar early."

Over the next few days the mission hall is transfixed into a small haberdashery unit, several sewing machines are utilised by the seamstress that Alice employs so that the charade is kept professional if any awkward questions are asked by the orphanages board members.

Later at home Alice writes a reply in earnest to the administrator, taking it down to the post office, to mark it special delivery

FOUR DAYS LATER

Inside the mission hall the girls are sombrely dressed, the seamstress are waiting at their machines, around the side of the hall, there are several old ladies, mothers with children sitting on chairs, Alice is by the window waiting for the car to turn up.

It duly arrives, Alice signals for all the group to start acting positively, Alice lets them in, the group disperse slowly walking around the hall, asking questions, picking up the dresses, the seamstresses come under scrutiny answering politely what they are doing, they take note of the prices, women with children.

After thirty minutes, the board members from their own group away from the girls, they beckon Alice over.

"Well Miss Diamond, your little enterprise is much more professional that we anticipated, we are pleasantly surprised at the workmanship, your offering to the local community, having said that we will fully endorse your application for the adoption."

"Thank you so much, I don't know what to say, would you like to stay for tea, cake, biscuits?"

"No, thank you all the same, we would not want to stop the hive of industry it has been very informative, goodbye."

They all shake hands.

Just before they leave, the matron nonchalantly looks at a dress on the mannequin, looks at the label 'Army and Navy' scrutinizes the dress again, looks at Alice, her facial expression changes.

"You know, I really thought I saw this dress quite recently."

She walks round pondering.

"Well maybe not."

"No Matron, this is very old stock,"

"Absolutely, goodbye,"

Alice waits until the group drive off in the car.

"Bloody hell girls, that was a close call."

Silence.

"Never mind, right Sandra, pay the extras, give 'em a bonus of a dress."

After the non-gang members had left, a quiet celebration was ordered.

A week later Alice received a letter stating that Rose was ready to be picked up at the orphanage.

On arrival Alice gets out three complete sets of baby clothes, lays them on the table, for Rose to choose from, decided, the Matron dresses her in them.

At Alice's house, the head administrator, the doctor look over her premises, taking note of the newly decorated babies' bedroom. After an hour of taking notes, asking questions they leave, Alice is in a quandary, she gently holds Rose on the sofa, Rose wriggles free, her attention taken by the large box of toys, contented she plays, Alice holds back her tear of emotion. A knock at the door, she gets up, goes to the door stops to turn to pick up Rose, they both go to the front door. Its Nora.

"Come in love, you're the first to meet our new member of the family.

Chapter 10

It's 1922. Alice is in a relationship with one of the Elephant Boys, she falls pregnant. This chain of events curtails her involvement with day to day running or organising her gang. After two months she marries Billy, the father. Other gangs have taken note of the success that the 'Forty Elephants' had achieved and wanted some of the action. This was to boil over at the theatre at the 'Elephant and Castle'.

To celebrate the marriage Billy had organised to take over the theatre for the enjoyment of the gang. It was to be a delayed surprise for Alice.

It was a well-kept secret within the 'Elephant' gang fraternity but an informer in the gang informed a North London gang.

This was their chance to get even over a grievance that has been festering for many weeks. In the car, Alice was told by Billy that they were going to a restaurant, telling her he was making amends by not taking her on a proper honeymoon.

On their arrival at the theatre Alice was overcome by the welcome, all her gang girl members formed a guard of honour at the entrance. Billy had booked the full-dress circle of the theatre, unbeknown to them the gang from North London were waiting in the stalls and the pits.

Everything was all quiet until the interval, Alice the entourage had gone up to the bar, Alice was with her girls, while Billy was small-talking to his associates. The last bell, the announcement for two minutes for the curtain call, the doors to the bar burst open. Pandemonium broke out, the intruders made a bee line for Billy's group, bottles in hand chains, chairs, anything that could bring injury was used, two of the girls pulled protesting Alice out through the fire exit, down the stairs to ground level, it took two more girls to hold her, in the bar, the fighting was vicious, in a close environment, protagonists, the innocents, succumbed to vicious wounds, the fight spread out to the door wells, down the corridors leading to the street when the North London gangsters who were not wounded or could walk, got into the motors, sped away, in the bar Billy's gang look around at the carnage, blood was everywhere, they found two of the gang, picked them up, unceremoniously hurled them through the doors, down the stairs, Billy is found slumped over a table, two men slowly pull him forward, he has a knife in his chest, they look at one another, he's dead.

The crowds outside the theatre hold up all the traffic in the street, the walking wounded get into their cars, the more serious are taken away in ambulances, to St. Thomas' hospital. Alice follows the convoy still not knowing the fate of Billy. The news was not good at the hospital. Billy was in the operating theatre. Alice is in the casualty department surrounded by her girls, the surgeon appears, walks over to Alice.

"I am sorry, he lost too much blood, a large shard of glass had punctured his lung and heart, he did not regain consciousness, there was no pain."

Alice collapse into the arms of the girls.

"Give her some air please."

The girls gently lie Alice down on the sofa.

A week after Billy's funeral Alice calls a meeting at the girls at her house., the parlour is crowded.

"Well girls I've got some news for you, I'm going to have Billy's baby."

The audience didn't know whether to laugh or cry, Alice broke the deadlock.

"Listen I want you to be happy for me, no tears, I'm going away for a few months, it'll do us all a favour, let the commotion die down a bit, you should all have enough money to carry on with if not you can dip in the emergency funds, don't get up to any mischief, an' keep out of trouble, the boys 'al look after you when I return I'll have a bonny baby to show yuh, now let's have a drink."

1925 EASTER

Alice, the gang had just entered a store in Regent Street, as always they were just about to split up, when one of the girls beckoned Alice's attention, over in the far corner of the store, there was another shoplifting gang, three girls were in the act of heisting some dresses, Alice gang looked her to see what her next move would be.

"Right girls, we cannot have this on our patch can we."

"It wouldn't do our reputation any good would it?"

"Right Alice."

"What I wanna do is let 'em carry on, wait till they get outside well' politely ask for a percentage."

"If they don't comply, we'll have to find some other means."

They break away from each other, wait for the other gang to get the dresses in their coats. Alice smiles at their movements, her girls are positioned by the exit doors, waiting for them to leave, Alice turns her back as they walk past her, wait for a few seconds then follows them out into the pavements, Alice nods to her girls to grab them, taken by surprise they try to protest but are hustled round the next corner, one of the kicks her captor in the shins losing her grip, the girl runs off, the other two are bundled into Alice's getaway car.

Alice is in the front sear turns around to confront her captives.

"Now I'm only going to ask you once, who are an what you doing working on our patch?"

Once of the girls starts to cry.

"It's too late for that deary! George stop at the next side street now I'm going to let one of you go I don't care who it is, but this is what's going to happen, when you get back you sort out your last month's money you made heisting, be ready by a phone, now which one of youse volunteering to stay?"

They both look at one another, the older one starts to cry.

"Let her go, she got kids at home, 'an the 'ole man knocks her about."

Alice pauses looking at the face acknowledging her loyalty.

"Right, that's settled then, you give her your dresses then she can go."

The older girl put the dresses in her bag kisses her friend, leaves the car, which pulls away.

Returning to Alice's house, the girl is hustled in.

"Right young lady, you'll be staying with us until the money comes across, don't try any funny stuff 'an you won't get harmed, alright?"

Alice, her girls get talking amongst themselves, the hostage has gained her composure starts to manicure nails.

"How long have you been in the game then?"

"About a year, better than working in the match box factory. I've seen so many girls suffer from diseases then dying, me and the girls you saw me with, we decided to try our hand at something else, we make a decent living at it."

"What's your name, how old are you?"

"Rose, seventeen years old."

The other gang members start to take an interest in the conversation.

"Who d'you give your money to when you get rid of the dresses, you got a minder?"

"Sort of, we supply the tat, the three of us split the money, he fences out the gear, everybody's happy."

"Okay, can you ring your minder? I'll put down on a piece of paper what I want you to say to 'im alright?"

After writing the note, she instructs the girl to phone.

"Allo Johnny, Its Rose, I'm in a bit of a pickle...she's told you already as she? Well I've been instructed to tell you that I'm going to be kept 'ere until you cough up the two hundred quid... he wants to know who you are."

"Just tell 'im I'm Alice Diamond."

"You still there Johnny? He said can he phone back in an hour?"

"Make it half an hour."

"He says alright."

"Are you the real Alice Diamond?"

"Yes, unless you know if I've got a twin – why the interest do you know me?"

"Well, us girls have heard a lot about you, Johnny showed us all the angles, how you went about your business, he used to take us out on test runs copying all your gangs techniques, 'an that, but I always remember telling us to be on the lookout for your gang, we made the mistake of intruding on your pitch."

"You certainly did young lady, you should have taken notice of 'im'."

After three quarters of an hour, the phone rings, Alice takes it, listens hands it over to Rose, she listens, puts the phone down, looks to Alice.

"He says e ain't got the money and I've got to take my chances."

Alice calls her girls into the back room.

"Wha'dyuh think we should do?"

"Well Alice if I was in her position how would I feel?"

"Why don't you give her a break, offer to work in our gang?"

"The thing is Alice we witnessed the way she works, she would need any more showing her the ropes an' she's probably got nowhere to go so she ain't gonna show the pimp any loyalty, would you?"

"You've made up your mind, you're a good bunch of girls."

They all go back into the other room.

"Right young lady you got two choices, one, you can leave now or two you can join our enterprise, what you wanna do?"

Rose looks round at the girls.

"I'll run with you Alice, if you give me a chance."

"Right that's settled then, I take it you've got nowhere to kip, so you can stay ere until we get you organised the girls' tell you how we operate, all I want is honesty 'n loyalty, right?"

Eight o'clock in the morning Sam quietly creeps up behind Fred car, taps on the window, Fred jumps spilling his flask over his clothes, Sam laughs carries walking towards 'The Cut'.

Sam's next rendezvous with McDonald was to be along the Embankment, the next day. The same procedure was followed; they both come from different directions to the gang-walk way to alight on a boat trip going towards the Isle of Dogs.

They take their different routes up to the front of the boat positioning themselves back to back.

"What's occurring?"

"Well after that blag, Rose mentioned that Alice's going to put her money into property, she realises the gang cannot go on forever without their collars being felt, an she's stating to let Rose make decisions."

"She's not as dumb as she looks, keeping it in the family like?"

"You could say, pity I'd like to have nicked her before she bows out."

"The thing is guv, we've got to nick 'er in the act, she too clever by far... I was meaning to ask you, have you got anybody giving any info to her, she seems a bit cagey towards me for some time you know when somebody doesn't trust you like, know what I mean?"

"Yuh I'll look into it."

Sam gets up, walks into the bar, leaving McDonald to admire the sights.

SUMMER

Rose, Sam have taken a trip to Brighton, they talk of marriage, Sam is reluctant to pursue the situation, at the back of his mind his involvement with the police force had to take paramount importance.

It was the morning of the last day, the pair were walking along the promenade, a couple walking towards him, it was too late, it was Jess, his friend in the force, he walks up to Sam goes to greet him.

"Hello Sam, long time no see, we heard…"

"Sorry mate, you must be mistaken, don think I know you."

Jess wouldn't take no for an answer.

"You always were one for a laugh, what you been up to?"

"Gonna introduce me to the young lady?"

"Listen pal I said you got the wrong fella, c'mon Rose."

Sam quickly walks away in the direction of the town, where they enter a bar.

"He was a bit pushy Sam, you sure you don't know him?"

"No Rose, now let it go."

"It just seems you must have a twin brother."

"That's about it."

On their return to London, Sam makes an excuse to Rose that he has to go to the bookies. In a phone box he rings Foden, explains the Brighton encounter.

"Whatever you do don't let 'im start to question my whereabouts, I getting to near to mess up Roses confidence, she's not stupid, 'an one of the gang is taking too much of an interest in me, if he links up with your brass in the force, my cover'll be blown."

Alice has decided to make one more raid then have a lay off. She was with Rose at a high class restaurant in the West End.

"Rose I've been thinking a lot lately about our situation, I'm beginning to feel the old age creeping up on me…"

"Don't say that Alice, you can still give a lot of our girls a run for their money."

"Don't you believe it, I've decided to go into semi-retirement, what I would like to do is for you to come with me on a little day out down to the Norwood, I've been looking at some magazine brochures and the look at the property, it's only a little way out, I want to get settled in before I get much older, you can take over the running of the gang, the girls would only be too pleased to work under you, besides it'll give you more time to spend with Sam."

"That's really nice of you Alice, but me 'n Sam were alright at the moment, were not putting any pressure on our relationship, maybe in the future we might tie the knot."

"Course you will, well you think about it, I'll have a word with Albert put him in the picture, he'll be alright putting you up from with the girls, … I would like one last poke at the summer sales, thought it could be my swan song."

"Yes, why not."

Sam is round Roses' flat, she mentions the conversation she had earlier with Alice, it wasn't until that Rose mentioned about her last blag, that she was going to retire, that Sam took an interest. It would be the last time that the police could arrest her in the act, he had to think fast.

"When's she thinking of doing it Rose?"

"Well the Regent Street sales start in a week's time, give us plenty of time, we gonna go for the big one again, were gonna raid four stores at once, it should even the odds, give us a better chance of getting away."

Sam takes it all in.

Next day Sam organizes a meet with Foden.

Fred, still suspicious of Sam's intentions goes round to Rose's flat.

"Sam about Rose, gotta talk a few things over about the job."

"No Fred, you just missed him, he's meeting the bookies runner down the Cut, if you hurry you'll catch."

Fred retraces his steps running through the flats, at the top end of 'The Cut' he catches sight of Sam.

Hess talking to the runner, Fred keeps back, Sam walks off to Waterloo station, Fred keeps in eyesight.

Inside the station, Sam walks up to the booking office, buys a platform ticket ? Fred waits, then goes up to the booking window.

"I'll have what the last geezer had."

"It was only a platform ticket."

"So what."

Fred is agitated waiting for Sam to make a distance between them he follows him. Sam goes through the barrier, he walks past two benches, looks round to see it the porter is looking, then jumps into an open door, to be seated next to Foden.

"They're going to go for the big one in a weeks' time; it's going to be Alice's last one, so you better make sure you got the man power to collar her, I'll contact you a day before, we don't want that grass getting the S.P. first."

Foden leaves first, Fred is behind a high loaded trolley of luggage, between a gap he recognizes Foden, waiting for him to leave, he sits on the bench opposite Sims door, appearing sever minutes later, Fred lets him get a distance between them, smiling walks away. Walking in the opposite directions he follows Foden leave the station, gets a cab on the rank, Fred follows in the next cab, the cab goes in a straight route to Scotland Yard. Fred watches Foden go into the building smiling: smiling self-satisfied with himself he leaves.

NEXT DAY MID MORNING

Alice, Rose are walking in a quiet street in Norwood, they observe the property Alice is interested in from across the road.

"Well what'd think of it Rose? It looked good on paper."

"Looks alright Alice, what time is the agent arriving?"

"He should be here now"

The agent shows the two around the house.

"Well ladies I hope it meets up to your approval, if there are any problems or questions, anything you're not sure of."

"No you've answered all my questions; I'll be getting in touch with you at the end of the week."

"Splendid."

On the train Alice is going through the brochure. "I've made up my mind Rose, I'm going for it."

"Good for you Alice, miss out little parties at the 'Eagle'"

"Never mind we'll have a big house warming keep the neighbours up for a night, only a one off." They laugh.

At the back of Albert's pub, he's going through the final directions of the raids.

"It'll be the same as the other big one, but with this one we've got advantages going our way, were going to hit Regents Street, Knightsbridge, Chelsea, also they got one of those kings visiting the palace. The police, manpower, security will put 'em full stretch, the roads should be clear for the most important thing of all is the timing, you've gotta all go in at the same time, confusion will be our best ally, now Fred'll dish out the drivers mates. Gets the cars tanked up check all the mechanics, I don't want any stalling down Oxford street, during the getaway."

Albert walks over to Alice. Rose says "Well Alice I'll be really sorry to see you retire, at least you're going out with a bang."

"I'm leaving it in very capable hands Albert. Rose is going to take over the operation. She'll be a credit to the 'Elephant Boys'."

"I'm sure she will Alice, she's had the best teacher in the business."

On the morning of the raid, Sam is with Alice in her flat. "Rose, you be careful with this one, it's a biggy, don't take any risks, get in, get out."

"What's the matter Sam, you're never usually like this? You're making me feel uncomfortable."

"No don't think like that, it's just the thought of Alice retiring, you taking over, it's a lot to take on your shoulders."

"Don't worry it'll be alright."

All the getaway cars are at their designated spots, the girls, enter the different stores, Sam is partnered up with Fred, the girls run out, jump into the getaway cars. Fred is quiet for a while then looks Sam straight in the eye, sarcastically.

"So how's your train spotting going Sam, if I'd known I would have joined yuh!"

"What you talking about?"

"You know what I'm talking about, I always thought you was a grass, when we get back I'll beat you so bad you'll need a show horn to put your hat on."

Fred goes for his gun, Sam has to fight him off with one hand on the wheel, the car hits the kerb swerves across the road, the girls scream, the car hits a coffee stall, Sam ducks just in time, Fred goes through the window hitting a bollard, dies instantly, the girls loot spills on to the road, the car behind pulls up they all get in.

"What about Fred?"

"What about Fred he's brown bread, let get out of 'ere!"

After putting distance from Oxford Street, the driver turns to Sam. "What happened there then, you was driving straight enough all of a sudden you smashed up?"

"Fred said I wasn't going fast enough, he tried to grab the wheel, I lost control."

"Funny Fred's was acting a bit strange lately."

"Do you know why?"

"Well he thought we had a grass in the camp, he was going to tell me an Albert after this little stint, well too late now, we'll never know."

Back at Alice's house, the cars return at different intervals, parking in different streets, the girls laden with the loot enter the parlour, Sam sits in the car lights a cigarette, pondering Rose comes out. "Sam it wasn't your fault, there's nothing you could have done."

He just looks at her. Alice and Albert are at the head of the table, the atmosphere is subdued.

"Right listen what I got to say, you've noticed Alice didn't take part in this blag, she pulled out at the last minute, you know why? We got a grass amongst us, the police had a plan to catch Alice in the act, but they came unstuck, now there's two ways we play this, one, Fred was going to tell me after this raid, he just wanted to fill in the last piece of the plot, now if any amongst you feel you have any loyalty to the gang I want you to write on these pieces of paper that Arnie will had round, Two, I'm gonna find out who it is, y'know why? Cause I got my own grass in the force, I'm meeting him tonight, he gonna tell me that all I'm gonna say at this point."

"How'd know you can trust this copper?"

"I know, he is so bent he jump through a keyhole."

"Right, I gotta make a little point, I've decided to retire to the suburbs, this way my last heist but I decided not to attend on Albert's say so, never the less, everything went according to plan except for the unfortunate situation of Fred, now I want you to raise your glasses to a friend who will be sorely missed… to Fred."

"I'll be handing over the leadership to Rose, Raise your glasses…Rose. I'll still be on hand in an adversary capacity if any of you girls need me."

The last words broke the ice, they all laughed.

"Well I'd like to say right here and now, nothing going to change, Alice will always be our spiritual leader you know that, so we'll take a little break from our dealing, let some of the rumpus cool down, enjoy yourselves, we'll have a divvy up in a couple of days."

Sam is taking this all in, he had to get his superior to tell him the news, he moves closer to Rose. "Congratulations Rose, it couldn't happen to a better lady."

"A better lady? Lady, your having a laugh ain't 'yuh?"

"No I mean it, maybe we can celebrate tonight?"

"That'll be nice. I don't suppose you have any inkling who it is, do you Sam?"

"Ain't got a clue Rose."

After an hour Sam made his excuses, telling Rose he'd pick her up at eight o'clock. He got a cab a short distance from his house, making sure he wasn't being followed, makes a phone call to Foden explaining about the grass.

"Don't worry, I know who it is, I plotted him up myself, he thought he was on to a winner, all what he told the 'Elephant Gang' I had a story to back it up, you never came into the frame but just be on the safe side, I'll get him seconded to the Vice Squad, first thing in the morning, you done good Sam, although we didn't Alice, at least she'll be off the streets, there ain't no one who can take her place… or is there?"

"Look I gotta go guv, that's what I gotta talk to you about."

On arrival at Roses flat, they decided to stay in. "So what d'yuh think of Alice's' announcement then Sam?"

"Well it took me right by surprise; I thought we had another ten years of her expertise."

"What don't y'think I make a good stand in then?"

"No, don't be silly, well it's just that I'm a bit worried something might happen to you."

"You old romantic."

"No straight up Rose, this grass were supposed to have in the gang, he could flare up anything, and when the old bill find out you're the main one in the frame, they're after you."

"Sam, it's the life I chose to take good, bad or indifferent, I just take my chances, like we all do. Don't be so melancholy let's have a drink."

A week later Alice moves into her house, there was a house warming a week later, the usual crowd attended much to the amazement of the peep curtain neighbours.

Sam didn't see Rose for a short while, she had to spend more time with Albert to get familiar with new ideas that he had in mind, Foden kept in touch with Sam, but at longer intervals.

After several weeks some of the girls in the gang take a leaf out of Alice's book. They all have their nest eggs, deciding that with more prosperity they were least tempted to a life of crime, moving out of trouble to the suburbs.

EPILOGUE

It is 1938. With the uncertainty of war in Europe, Sam finds himself in the position of not knowing which way his life is heading. He talks it over with Rose, deciding he is going to join the forces. They agree to get married.

A year later they have a baby girl.

At the outbreak of war, Sam is called up to serve in the Royal Tank regiment. For Rose this is going to be the next chapter in her life...

Printed in Great Britain
by Amazon